About the

Emily Smith had what she calls a
her book, *The Shrimp*, was av   ᴜ une Smarties
Gold Award in 2001. "I was surprised then, and I am
still surprised!" says Emily. She has also been
shortlisted for the Blue Peter Prize (but, to her
great disappointment, was not given a Blue Peter
Badge). *A Stain on the Stone* is Emily's third title for
Orchard Books. Emily lives with her husband and
three children in Oxfordshire.

For M
With grateful thanks to OT

St Luke's College is imaginary.
So are all the people in this book.
Oxford, of course, is a real place.

ORCHARD BOOKS
338 Euston Road, London NW1 3BH
Orchard Books Australia
Level 17-207 Kent Street, Sydney, NSW 2000, Australia
ISBN 978 1 84616 210 7
First published by Orchard Books in 2006
This paperback edition first published in 2007
Text © Emily Smith 2006
The right of Emily Smith to be identified as the author
of this work has been asserted by her in accordance with
the Copyright, Designs and Patents Act, 1988.
A CIP catalogue record for this book is available from the British Library.
1 3 5 7 9 10 8 6 4 2
Printed in Great Britain
www.orchardbooks.co.uk

Orchard Books is a division of Hachette Children's Books

a JACK
YOUNG
mystery

A STAIN
on the
STONE

EMILY
TH

BOOKS

CONTENTS

1

A Shock for Mr McGuffin

One morning, early in term, Joe McGuffin was walking round the cloisters of St Luke's College.

Mr McGuffin was head of works at the famous Oxford College. He knew and loved every building of St Luke's. He loved the very old bits, the less old bits, and was even quite fond of the concrete student block right on the road.

But his pride and joy were the cloisters. They were old. They were beautiful. Mr McGuffin could never decide which side was more beautiful, the north side, the south side, the west side or the east side.

Mr McGuffin protected those cloisters. If any students dared to stick up posters for plays or discos, these were removed at once, and the stickers-up hunted down. They did not do it again. And no piece of litter ever lay for long *on the neatly mown lawn in the centre.*

Soon after 8 am, Mr McGuffin was walking along the north side, when he saw, straight ahead of him, something on the wall.

It made his heart beat faster.

It made his mouth fall open.

It made his eyes pop.

2

New Wheels

Jack Young had a new bike.

It was a great bike.

It had the right handlebars. The right gears. The right tyres. It was a bike any fourteen-year-old would be proud of.

His friend Marco took one look and burst into Italian (he was half Italian). *"Che bella macchina!"* What a beautiful machine.

"It is," said Jack. "Isn't it?" He locked the bike, double-checked the lock, and leant back on the railing to admire it. "But now I have no money."

"So?" said Marco. "What do you need money for?"

"Carrie's birthday," said Jack.

There was silence.

"I'd lend you some," said Marco.

"I know," said Jack.

"But I don't have any."

"I know," said Jack.

"Carrie's quite little," Marco said. "You could give her one of your things. Wrap it up nicely."

"Mmm. No," said Jack.

Another silence.

Suddenly Marco lit up. "I know!"

Jack knew at once what was coming.

"Why don't you *make* her something?"

Make her something!

What sort of suggestion was that?

Jack thought about it as he biked home after school.

Make her something!

Yes, OK, adults liked being made things. Or so they said. But little girls? Little girls liked things made of pink and mauve plastic with lots of wrapping that came from shops. And things made of pink and mauve plastic with lots of wrapping that came from shops cost money…

Make her something!

What a dumb idea!

The only trouble was, Jack had no others.

Then he forgot about Carrie's present, and just enjoyed his bike. What a beautiful machine! *Che bella macchina!* It was as smooth as…ice-cream…

The bike lane was quite busy. A girl had stopped to answer her mobile phone – he wished people wouldn't do that! He passed her, then slowed down behind a large woman with lots of shopping in her basket. Then a beefy student in games kit overtook them both.

When he got home, he wheeled his bike up the side alley, and locked it. He walked into the house, swinging his helmet in his hands.

There was no one in. Mum was still at work at St Luke's, and Carrie was with her minder.

He kicked off his shoes, and walked in his socks to the kitchen. Then he flung open the fridge, and peered in.

Hmm, disappointing. The best bet was a bowl of cold roast parsnips. Jack took a parsnip from the bowl. He thought of Marco's fridge. There was nearly always home-made pasta in Marco's fridge. The boys had been known to eat it cold.

Jack sighed.

What do Italian mums keep in the fridge? Spaghetti Bolognese.

What do English mums keep in the fridge? Cold roast parsnips.

No contest, really.

Jack took another cold parsnip…

He started his homework.

Mum rang. "Are you there?" she said.

"Yes," said Jack. "If I wasn't, I couldn't answer the phone."

Mum laughed, and asked about his homework. "It sounds interesting," she said.

"It's not," said Jack.

"*Quite* interesting, then."

"It's not."

"Well, it'll teach you something."

"It won't," said Jack.

"Oh," said Mum.

He had nearly finished his homework, when he looked at his clock and realised his programme was on. It had been on for five minutes.

He leapt up, ran down the stairs, jumped the last three steps and landed on something hard. Ooof! His foot hurt!

He sat, rubbing his foot and looking around. *That* was what he had landed on. He picked it up. It was one of Carrie's rabbits. Peter, probably.

How could a little thing like that hurt so much?

What was Peter doing lying at the foot of the stairs?

Why couldn't Carrie stop her rabbits going everywhere?

And then Jack had his idea. He would make Carrie a house for her rabbits.

3

Oxford Blue

"Well, if you go to the Covered Market, could you get some Oxford Blue?"

"*What?*" said Jack.

"Oxford Blue," said Mum said. "It's cheese."

The supermarket was no good. It only had brown cardboard boxes. Jack wanted something better than that. He biked down to the centre, and into Broad Street. He liked the Broad, because there was very little traffic and plenty of room. It was so clear, in fact, that he tried a wheelie. The front wheel cleared beautifully.

He turned down a side street, and spotted a shoe shop. He braked to a halt to get a better look. In the window was a display of fine leather shoes. *Hmm*, Jack thought. *What about a shoe-box?*

He left his bike by a wall and went back to the window.

There were rows of gleaming brown and black shoes. Real leather ones, like the Master of St Luke's wore. But he could not see any shoe-boxes. Right at the side were some tins of shoe-polish. They were round, with little levers to lift the lids off.

Jack started reading the colours on the tins. *Black, light brown, dark brown, blue, neutral* and…what was the last colour? *Ox…blood?* Surely that could not be right? Jack moved closer to check. It was right.

Ox blood? Jack gazed at the colour on the tin lid. It was not really blood colour, more browny-red.

Did oxes – *oxen* – really have blood that colour?

Did the shoe-polish have *real* blood in it?

If so, did they kill the ox, or just…?

He peered behind the display into the shop. He could not see much.

He decided to go in.

But just as he reached the door, the door opened, and a man swept out. A tall, elegant man, in a brown hat. He met Jack's gaze for a second, then turned and set off towards the High Street.

Suddenly Jack changed his mind. He would try the Covered Market first.

Jack liked the Covered Market. It was fun, walking down the old-fashioned alleyways, with all the different stalls and shops. There was something new at every turn.

He wandered around. The smell of coffee was overtaken by the smell of flowers, which was overtaken by the smell of fish. Jack chose which jeans he would buy if he had any money. He admired the rack of different-coloured keys at the key-cutters, and read the notice about which days buskers were allowed. And suddenly he found himself looking at a little shop he'd never seen before.

It was a hat shop.

There were wonderful hats on display. They were hats to wear to a garden party or a wedding or the races. They had ribbons and bows and feathers and netting and some even had cherries on the brim. One looked like a chocolate pudding.

Hats…

Big hats.

And big hats came in…big hat boxes…

Jack stepped inside the little shop. A smartly-dressed woman came forward. "Can I help you?"

"I wonder if I could possibly have a hat box?" said Jack.

The woman raised her eyebrows.

"I need to make something for my sister."

The smartly-dressed woman pursed her lips. "Are you one of our regular customers?"

Jack stared at her. Did he *look* the sort of person who'd buy a hat like a chocolate pudding?

Then he saw a twinkle in her eye.

"No," he said, "I'm not."

"Wait here," she said. "I'll see what I can find." She went through a little door at the back of the shop, and within seconds came back holding a big square white box.

Jack looked at it.

It was perfect.

It would make not just a rabbit house. It would make a rabbit palace!

Grinning his thanks, he took the box and carried it away.

It was only when he was walking out of the market that he remembered.

Mum's cheese!

He had nearly forgotten Mum's cheese.

He made his way to the cheese stall.

There was one person being served. He was tasting lots of different cheeses to put together "an amusing cheese board" for his dinner party. Jack held the big white box to his chest. He didn't want to put it on the ground.

While he was waiting, he watched people go by.

A man in a brown hat walked past, carrying a bag from the coffee shop. He seemed familiar. Of course! He was the man coming out of the shoe shop…

"Yes?" said a voice.

Jack turned to see the girl behind the cheese counter.

"What would you like, sir?"

Jack frowned. *What had Mum asked for?*

"I want some…cheese," he said.

"Yes." The girl smiled. "What sort of cheese would you like?"

Jack gazed at the array of cheese before him. The queue of customers was getting bigger. He decided to play for time.

"What *is* cheese?"

The girl looked taken aback, and suddenly Jack realised that she was younger than he had thought. She was about his age, or a bit older. She frowned. "Well, it's basically…it's…fermented milk."

Another customer spoke up. "Actually I'm not sure fresh cheese *is* fermented."

"It is!" said someone else. "Fresh cheese is fermented, but not *ripened*."

A man rolled his eyes, and looked at his watch.

A woman tutted, and said. "Only in Oxford!"

"Blue!" shouted Jack.

4

Blood-Red Letters

The packet of Oxford Blue (a neatly-cut 200 grams) fitted snugly into the pocket of Jack's jacket. As long as he didn't fall on it, the cheese was not a problem.

The cheese was not a problem.

But the box *was*.

Jack looked at his bike, and realised he couldn't possibly get the box home on it.

Then he remembered something. Mum had taken the car to St Luke's that day. Something to do with driving the Master somewhere. Jack decided to go to the college, and get a lift home with her.

He double-checked his bike lock, lifted the box high on his chest, and set off down the High Street.

There were many fine and famous buildings on the left-hand side of the street, but Jack didn't glance at them. There were many fine and famous buildings on the right-hand side of the street, but Jack didn't glance at them either. He was thinking about his rabbit house.

At the corner with St Luke's Lane, Jack waited for a chance to cross. When a gap appeared in the traffic, he stepped into the road.

The next second a van rounded the corner, and hurtled towards him.

Jack leapt back quickly. He very nearly dropped the box. The van sped past, missing him by centimetres.

Heart thudding, Jack gazed after it. The van was speeding away down St Luke's Lane, indicating right. That was strange. The only right near there was into St Luke's car park. Surely the badly-driven van was not going there? But, yes! The van slowed, and turned right through the gates. He watched it disappear from sight.

Jack took his time crossing the lane, then walked on. He was soon stepping through the little door of the main entrance to St Luke's.

In front of him was a "College Closed to Public" sign.

"*Yes?*" said a voice from the porter's lodge.

Jack turned. It wasn't Bill, the porter who sometimes took him fishing. It was a young porter he didn't know. Behind him Jack could see the shifting screens of the CCTV monitors.

"I'm Mrs Young's son," said Jack.

The porter nodded him through, and Jack walked on, into the paved area called Front Quad.

As he crossed Front Quad, he lifted the white box higher on his chest. It was not heavy, but it was getting awkward to carry. He passed through an archway, and was two steps into Ox Quad, when he bumped into someone.

This was a student in sports kit, who had been walking along, talking loudly. He looked down in surprise at Jack, and said, "Hey!"

"What are you *doing*, Alex?" said an amused voice from above.

"I've just bumped into somebody!" Alex called up.

"Well, don't!" A blonde girl was standing at a first floor window.

"It was because I was talking to you!" said Alex.

The girl laughed. "Luke's students are supposed to be able to walk and talk at the same time!"

Jack just stood there while they talked.

Finally Alex looked down at him. "Is your box all right?"

"Yes," said Jack.

"Good!" said Alex. "There's nothing worse than having one's box damaged."

Then he laughed, and looked up. "Right, then! I'm off to mash St Peter's!" And he was gone.

To cross Ox Quad, Jack walked along a path which

made two sides of a square. The quickest way was to go over the grass in the middle, but only senior members of college were allowed on that.

Two elderly dons were strolling across it now.

One of them was rather deaf.

Or perhaps both of them were rather deaf.

Jack could hear every word.

"Is that an undergraduate, Cecil? It looks rather small for an undergraduate."

"Sometimes they are small, Alfred. I had a very small one once. Brilliant historian."

"It is carrying something, Cecil. Can you see what it is carrying?"

"Yes, Alfred. A large white cube."

"A large white cube?"

"A large white cube."

"*Why* is it carrying a large white cube?"

"Your guess is as good as mine, Alfred."

"I never guess, Cecil. You know that."

"If you say so, Alfred."

"Shall we go to primary sources?"

"Always the safest, Alfred."

The two dons had now left the grass square, and were standing at the corner by the entrance to the cloisters.

"Excuse me?" said Cecil politely, as Jack approached.

"Yes?" said Jack.

"Would you satisfy our curiosity," said Cecil, "and tell us why you are transporting that object through college?"

"What?" said Jack.

"What is the white cube for?"

"*Oh!*" said Jack. "I'm going to make a house for rabbits."

The elderly dons did not seem surprised.

"A house for rabbits," repeated Cecil gravely.

"Rabbits," said Alfred.

"Well, well!"

"Heh, heh!"

"Rabbits, eh?"

"Rabbits."

They thanked Jack politely, and moved off towards the cloisters.

Jack followed the two dons through the archway into the cloisters, deciding that, whichever way they went round, he would go the other.

The dons turned to the right, so Jack turned to the left.

He walked along, his eyes drawn to the sunlit grass square in the middle. But as he neared the second corner, he saw something strange.

There were two metal barriers set in front of the wall at about waist height. Yellow tape was stuck

22

along the top of the barriers. There was plenty of room to walk past the barriers, but it looked odd.

Like a crime scene, almost.

But if this was a crime scene, what was the crime?

Then Jack drew nearer, and saw it. About half a metre above the top of the barriers, someone had written something.

Jack stood and stared.

They seemed to be letters – weird letters.

Written in blood.

The blood gleamed redly, a stain on the cloister wall. What was the blood from? An animal? An ox? A *human*? Suddenly the air seemed cold.

Then another thought struck him. Not blood from an ox, perhaps, but what about blood from a smaller animal? Like Maisie, the college cat? Surely not! No one would harm Maisie!

Then his scalp started to prickle.

And suddenly he *knew* someone was standing right behind him

He spun round.

There was no one at person level.

He looked down.

"*Miaow?*" said Maisie.

5

The Professor

"Maisie!" cried Jack. "You're OK!" He bent down, and stroked her.

"*Miaow!*" Maisie nuzzled his pocket.

"That's blue cheese, Maisie! Cats don't like blue cheese!"

"*Prrrp!*"

"You're a clever girl, though!"

Maisie gave a little shake of the head, then trotted on.

Jack turned back to the writing in blood. There were three letters. Or symbols. The first was a big cross, like a capital 'X'. The second was a strange letter, with lots of curls and turnings to it. The last letter was the most familiar. It looked like an 's'.

Somehow the letters did not seem random. They

obviously meant *something*. But what? They were not like any graffiti Jack had seen before.

He stared for a bit, then gave up. Hoisting the box higher in his arms, he walked the few metres on to Mum's office. The outer door, directly opening into the cloisters, was open. The inner door was closed. Jack turned the handle, and walked in.

Mum was at her desk, holding a phone to her ear with one hand, and tapping her keyboard with the other. Beside her was a pile of office files. In the corner the fax was printing something out. She looked harassed.

"Yes, I'll hang on!" she said into the phone. "But please tell him it's urgent!" Frowning, she swung round in her chair. "*Jack!*" she cried. It was not the most welcoming of 'Jacks'.

"I came because I couldn't get this on my bike." Jack put the box on her desk. It was a relief to put it down.

Mum did not ask what the box was for.

She didn't even look at it properly.

She just sort of frowned at it.

Jack moved the box to the floor by the wall.

"Still holding!" said Mum into the phone. Then she covered it, and spoke to Jack. "Well, you'll have to wait! We've got a crisis on!"

"Yes," said Jack. "I saw it!"

"You *saw* it?"

"The writing in the cloisters!"

Mum rolled her eyes. "Oh, that! That's not the main crisis. But that's appalling, isn't it?"

"Yes! Weird!"

"Mr McGuffin is *not* happy!"

"But where do you think the blood came from?" said Jack.

"Blood?" Mum looked blank. "I don't think— "

Suddenly she was talking into the phone again. "He *can't* speak now? But you said—"

She listened a bit, then sighed. "All right, I'll try then." She put the phone down with a sigh.

Just then a middle-aged man in a jacket and tie came in.

"Hello, Professor Baker!" Mum smiled at him "Back from London?"

"Yes!" The professor put his briefcase down.

"Lecture go well?" Mum said.

Professor Baker smiled. "I think so!" He leaned slightly over Mum's desk. "Anything further happened on the...um...?" he asked.

"Well..." Mum glanced at Jack. Just then a buzzer went on her phone, and she picked it up.

The voice that came through on her phone, though faint, was unmistakeable. It was the gravelly tones of the Master of St Luke's.

Mum listened for a few seconds, then said, "Not at all, Master." She pulled a file from the pile on her desk. "I've got it here. Do you want it now?"

While she was talking on the phone, Professor Baker looked at Jack. "Are you Mrs Young's son?"

Jack nodded.

"I knew she had a young family." He smiled at Jack. "She does a fantastic job here, you know."

Pleased, Jack smiled back.

"Jack?" Mum had her hand over the phone, and was looking at him.

"Yes?"

Mum held the blue file towards him. "Could you take this to the Master's Lodgings?"

"Er..."

"Please?"

"OK."

He took the file, and set off towards the Master's Lodgings.

He could have gone the other way, but he went past the corner where the red letters were.

There was something about them that drew him.

Holding the file to his chest, he stared at the writing again.

Was it written in blood?

Or something else?

Suddenly he noticed something he hadn't seen before.

Here and there the red colour had pooled slightly. Not enough to drip, just enough to make little bulges of darker red. Mostly in the lower parts of the letters.

Was it really blood?

It was more like…

Suddenly he had the feeling there was someone behind him again.

Maisie?

He turned round, eyes at cat level.

No Maisie.

No cat at all.

But there *were* some legs.

Human legs.

His eyes travelled up.

It was Professor Baker.

Jack was just about to say something, when he noticed the look on his face.

Professor Baker was staring at the three letters.

And – was it Jack's imagination – or had he gone pale?

6

The Master's Lodgings

"Balliol!" said a high voice behind them.

The professor and Jack spun round.

It was Cecil.

The professor frowned. "What do you mean, Balliol?"

Cecil nodded his head at the red letters. "They did it, I bet!"

"Balliol? *Why?*"

"They don't have cloisters!" said Cecil.

The professor sighed. "Lots of Oxford colleges don't have cloisters, Cecil. In fact *most* Oxford colleges don't have cloisters."

Cecil made an obstinate face. "Well, have you got a better theory?"

Professor Baker did not answer.

Cecil looked at the red letters, and shook his head.

Jack walked on towards the Master's Lodgings.

The Lodgings were large and imposing. As Jack got nearer, they got larger and even more imposing. He walked up a short flight of steps, and found the big wooden door closed tight. He looked around for somewhere he could post the file. There was nothing. Nowhere you could even post a small envelope. He examined the bottom of the door. A tight fit. Very tight.

There was no hope for it. Jack rang the bell. Maybe there was a smiley housekeeper or someone who would open the door? Yes, Jack liked the idea of a smiley housekeeper...

While he waited, he glanced at the blue file. It was labelled, 'Old Lecture Hall'. It did not look interesting.

Suddenly the door swung inwards.

Jack looked up – straight into the Master's eyes.

They were grey and appraising.

"I've brought a file!" Jack thrust it into the Master's stomach. "From Mrs Young!" And he darted off.

The white box sat on the back seat of the car.

"We're running a bit late," said Mum, turning into the traffic.

He ought to make a second floor.

"We can fetch Carrie afterwards."

Maybe it should only go halfway across.

"Debbie said it was fine."

A staircase too, of course…

The car went over a hump.

It wasn't the first hump either.

Hey! There were no humps on the way home!

Jack sat up. "Where are we going?"

"The station," said Mum.

"The station?"

"I *told* you! To pick up Aunt Polly!"

"Oh!" Jack frowned. "I forget what you said exactly."

"Well…" said Mum. "Aunt Polly is my aunt. Your great-aunt."

"Yes."

"She's just retired from her job."

"Yes."

"And I've asked her to stay for a week or so."

"Right…"

"That's why I asked you to get the Oxford Blue."

"Ah," said Jack. "I wondered about that…"

Aunt Polly. Aunt *Polly. Aunt…Polly.*

Jack thought he remembered her vaguely from a family wedding. A grey-haired woman. Glasses, possibly.

Oh, well, Jack thought.

Aunt Polly wouldn't be much fun.

But she wouldn't be any trouble, either.

He was wrong on both counts.

7

Aunt Polly

"I can't see her anywhere!" Mum peered at the people streaming through the barrier. Then she gasped. "Oh, my goodness!"

The person standing in front of them was not the woman Jack remembered. She was not grey-haired for a start.

Her hair was bright red.

Her clothes were bright too.

All sorts of bright colours.

"Wow!" Mum kissed her aunt. "You look fantastic!"

"Thank you, Annie!" Aunt Polly gave a happy smile. "It's my new look!"

Jack offered to carry her case.

"How kind!" said Aunt Polly. "But it's more

trundling than carrying!" She pulled out some wheels.

Jack trundled the case to the car.

Aunt Polly sat in the front with Mum.

Jack sat in the back with his box.

As they drove out of the station, Aunt Polly peered around eagerly. "I can't believe I've never been to Oxford! This is so exciting! Point out the sights, Jack! What's that?" She pointed to a modern building with a green stepped tower on the roof.

"It's...um, part of the university," said Jack.

Mum laughed. "Good guess, Jack! It's the business school."

"That's a fine bronze!" Aunt Polly pointed to a sculpture of a large animal. "What is it?"

"Looks like a bull," said Jack.

"Close!" said Mum. "I'll give you a clue. We're in Oxford."

"Um..."

"An ox?" said Aunt Polly.

"Yup!" said Mum.

"Is that how Oxford got its name?" said Aunt Polly. "The place where ox forded the river?"

"Yup!" Mum swerved to avoid a cyclist.

"Well, it's a good thing it wasn't where pigs forded the river," said Aunt Polly. "Or you'd be living in Pigford."

He should not have run downstairs so quickly.

Not without taking his jacket off.

It was just that he wanted to hide the box in his room, and then get down to the fridge. Fast. It is much easier to raid a fridge without a great-aunt in the kitchen.

As he came running back down the stairs, his feet got muddled up.

Both landed on the same step at the same time, which should have been fine. But was not.

Jack lost control.

He fell heavily to the foot of the stairs.

As he got up, he felt something squidge in his jacket pocket.

The Oxford Blue took up the whole cheese board.

"It tastes fine," said Aunt Polly at supper. "It doesn't affect the taste at all."

"And it goes further," said Mum. "Being flat."

Aunt Polly cut herself some more. "Sure you don't want some, Jack?"

Jack nodded. "I'm not a great blue cheese person."

"Are you not a great blue cheese person?" said Aunt Polly.

"No," said Jack.

8

Stolen!

This could not be happening.

This could NOT be happening.

Jack stared at the space where his bike had been.

There was no bike.

His bike had gone.

His bike was no longer there.

His amazing new bike.

Jack's heart was hammering.

He knew it was the right spot because of the lamppost. His bike had been attached to the lamppost with the bikelock, just as you were supposed to.

He looked desperately up and down the row of bikes, leaning against the wall. None of the bikes was his.

Jack gave a moan. Of course his bike had gone.

It was so beautiful! How could it not go? How could he have been so stupid! To leave it overnight in town?

He gave another moan.

"Are you OK?"

He looked up to see a girl. She was wheeling a bike down the road.

"No!" he said. "I'm not!"

"Oh!" she said. There was something familiar about her.

"I've had my bike stolen."

She made a face. "Oh, no! Are you sure?"

He nodded.

The girl looked up and down the street. "It's terrible," she said. "*They're* terrible. There've been a lot of bikes stolen recently."

"Really?"

She nodded. "My uncle had his stolen last month, but it was an old one."

"Mine was new," said Jack. "It was…" He trailed off.

"I'm sorry," said the girl.

There was silence for a second or two.

"So what are you going to do?" said the girl. "Report it to the police?"

"Suppose." Somehow reporting it to the police would mean the bike had really gone. Was he ready for that?

36

"Have one last look up and down the street," said the girl. "And then I'll give you a lift to the police station."

"A lift? Have you got a car?" said Jack.

"No! Of course not!" And the girl nodded at her bike.

It was not very comfortable on the carrier.

In fact it was very uncomfortable.

But the girl pedalled off confidently, and Jack kept his feet up and held on to the saddle.

The girl took a right, then pedalled on down the street.

"Are you OK?" she shouted back.

"No!" Jack shouted back. "I've had my bike stolen!"

He stared at the back of the girl's crash helmet. Where had he seen her before? School? No. The Burger bar? No. Ice-rink? No. So where…?

The girl swerved to the left, neatly avoiding a group of tourists. Jack saw several holding up cameras, and wondered what they were taking photos of. Then the girl took a right up the High Street.

A bus hooted.

"Hang on!" said the girl, as she steered left at Carfax. "Not far now!"

Jack hung on.

She sped down St Aldate's, past a great college.

A porter in a bowler hat watched them with a frown.

Was it a general frown – at the world?

Or a particular frown – at them?

Jack was not sure.

Finally, the girl drew to a stop outside the big red-brick police station. "Here you are, Sir!" She grinned round at him. "The nick!"

Jack eased himself off. "Right!"

"You go round the back, I think." The girl pointed down the side.

"Oh. Right."

"I'll be off then!"

"OK. Thanks."

He gave her a nod, and turned.

He knew now where he'd seen her before.

He knew it as soon as she'd grinned and said, "Sir."

She was the girl who had sold him 200 grams of Oxford Blue…

9

'Buck House'

"Did they think you'd get it back?" said Marco.

"I didn't ask," said Jack.

"Oh," said Marco. "I'd have asked."

Jack shrugged.

"You didn't have it very long, did you?"

"No," said Jack.

"How long was it? Four days?"

"Marco?" said Jack.

"What?"

"Shut up, will you?"

"OK."

There was silence.

"I expect you could borrow my sister's bike."

"What's it like?" said Jack.

"It's old and rusty and it clanks a bit."

"Oh."

"It's fine."

Jack measured the door and windows carefully, and cut them out on the kitchen table. Aunt Polly painted two of the walls, and stuck down the carpets (made from an old shirt).

They finally decided on a name, and Jack wrote 'BUCK HOUSE' in black ink over the door, and drew a carrot each side. He also cut out a little letter-box, and wrote 'LETTERS' on it. Last of all he stuck on a satellite dish (a bit of bicycle bell).

When Carrie opened her present, Jack felt quite proud.

"A 'ouse!" said Carrie brightly. "A little 'ouse!"

"It's a rabbit house," said Jack. "For your rabbits."

Carrie gave a crow of delight. "It's gotta bell!"

"Well, that's really a sat—"

"Ping!" cried Carrie, pretending to flick the bell.

"Oh. OK. Ping!"

"Ping!" said Carrie. "Ping, ping, ping!"

"And this is Ox Quad," said Mum.

"It's *beautiful*!" Aunt Polly gazed round at the honey-coloured stone. "What a wonderful place to work!"

"Yes," said Mum. "And no."

Aunt Polly shot her a glance. "Really?"

Mum gazed around the quad. "Believe me, it gets stressful at times."

Carrie was whining, and pulling at Mum's hand. She was not a fan of old stones.

"Look, Carrie!" Aunt Polly pointed to a stone relief over an archway. "Look at the animal! What do you think it is?"

Carrie glanced up without much interest. "Is it a wabbit?"

"Well…no," said Aunt Polly. "I don't think it is a rabbit." She peered at it. "Could it be a horse?"

"Not in Ox Quad," said Mum.

"Oh, an ox!" said Aunt Polly.

"Yes." Mum nodded. "The ox is a symbol of St Luke. There are several round the college, if you look."

"Really?" said Aunt Polly.

"Yes," said Mum. "And lots of gargoyles! Though you need binoculars to see some of them properly."

Aunt Polly looked thoughtful.

"Come on!" said Mum. "Let's go to the chapel! I've got the key."

They went round the south side of the cloisters. Jack glanced across the lawn. "Are those red letters still there?"

"All gone, thank goodness!" said Mum.

"Still no idea who did it?"

Mum shook her head.

Aunt Polly admired everything. She admired the cloisters. She admired the antechapel. She admired the chapel.

Jack trailed after them. He had seen the chapel before. It looked the same as it did last time. It smelt the same too. And his feet sounded the same on the tiled floor.

Carrie thought there ought to be singing in the chapel. So she sang "One Green Bottle." It was a good thing there was no one else around. Jack told her there was a dead body in the wall under a plaque, which kept her quiet for a bit. Then she started up again. "One geen body, sittin' in der wall!"

"Would you like to see the Old Library now?" said Mum, as she closed the wooden studded door of the antechapel.

"Oh, *yes!*" said Aunt Polly.

Jack sighed. Anything old, and she was away! Aunt Polly would probably be keen to see an old *toilet*!

"What about you, Jack?" said Mum.

"No," said Jack.

"What will you do then?"

"I'll wait in the cloisters," said Jack.

He did.

First he looked at the place where the red letters

had been. Mr McGuffin, or whoever it was, had done a good job cleaning up. There was a slightly light patch where the letters had been. But unless you knew where to look, you wouldn't notice it.

Jack leant against the wall, and waited.

At one stage a group of students came noisily past. It looked as though they had just been to a meeting or something.

One of them was Alex, the student he had bumped into when carrying the white box. Alex had his arm round one girl, and was laughing and chatting with another.

The students clattered on by.

It was quiet again.

Jack stared at his feet.

A leaf had blown in to rest on a flagstone.

He moved the leaf gently with the tip of his trainer, and found himself staring at a red spot.

10

The Red Spot

The red spot gleamed.

Jack looked at it. It seemed to look back at him.

The spot was round, about a centimetre in diameter. It was the same blood-red colour as the letters on the wall.

Jack knelt down, and touched it with his finger. It was hard. If it had ever been liquid, it was now quite dry. He tried to get it off with his nails, but could not shift it. Jack put a hand in his pocket, and found a coin. It was his only coin. A two pence piece. He pushed it to the edge of the red spot. It came away neatly, in one piece.

Jack got to his feet slowly, examining the red spot.

It was not blood. It was blood-coloured, but it was not blood. It was more like…paint.

Paint! Of course! It had never been blood on that wall! It was paint! And whoever had done it had spilt a drop right here. And why?

Jack knew why.

The archway nearby led out to a passage, and that passage led towards the works department...

To start with, Jack was just looking for more red spots.

He walked through the archway, and down the passage without seeing any. He came out in a little courtyard between buildings, with a small tree in the middle.

He gazed around. He couldn't quite remember the way to the works department. There were three different exits. The left exit would lead to the car park, and probably the Fellow's Garden. Towards the right loomed the concrete block that housed most of the first-year students. He moved to one side so he could look past the tree and down the alley straight ahead. *Bingo!* There, at the bottom, was the brick face of the works department.

He walked on down, checking the ground.

No red spots.

As he got nearer, he saw that the door was ajar. The latch, which was the sort that takes a padlock, was hanging loose.

Jack went up to the door. "Mr McGuffin?" he called.

There was no sound.

"Mr McGuffin?" He called a bit louder.

Still no sound.

Jack knew he shouldn't go in.

But he was excited about the red spot.

He was on a trail.

He pulled the door open a bit more and stepped inside.

The room was fairly large, but only had one window. At first Jack could hardly make anything out in the gloom. Then his eyes began to adjust.

He had a shock when he spotted the dead body.

It was under a dustsheet on a bench by the wall.

He stared at it.

Was it really a dead body?

Was *that* why Mr McGuffin hadn't answered?

There were a lot of lumps under the dust-sheet.

Maybe it was not a dead body. Maybe it was two dead bodies.

Mr McGuffin and somebody else?

Jack stood and stared at the lumps a bit more. But standing and staring was getting him nowhere. He walked slowly up to the dust-sheet, took hold of a corner, and drew it back.

He was looking at a lathe. Next to it was another machine – something like a grinder. He almost laughed. What an idiot he was! The machines were nothing like dead bodies! He put the dust-sheet back.

He took another look round the room. He could see better now. To one side lay some metal step-ladders. Over there was a cement-mixer. But where was the paint kept?

At the far side of the room was a door, which was nearly closed. Jack walked over, and pulled it open. His gaze fell upon a large walk-in cupboard with shelves on all three sides. There were tools, rolls of wire, and buckets. There was plumbing stuff. Electrical stuff. And decorating stuff. On one side were two rows of paint cans.

Jack stepped in, and started looking over the paint cans. The first can was white gloss. So was the second. And the third. There was a lot of magnolia. There was even a pot of gold. Jack wondered where that was used. The chapel? There was black paint too. And something called 'anti-climb' paint. But there was no blood-red paint.

The nearest thing was a tin of something for treating wood (there was a lot of wood at St Luke's). But Jack looked at the brownish dribble down the side, and decided it was not red enough.

Jack had just finished checking the final can when

he heard a noise behind him.

It was a scraping sort of noise.

A metallic noise.

Not the sort of noise you want to hear when you're alone in a dark and unfamiliar place.

Someone – or something – was behind him.

11

'Help!'

Jack spun round. No one was behind him.

No one was in the cupboard. No one, as far as he could see, was in the outside room.

He stepped out into it, heart thumping.

He was right. There was no one in the room.

But something had changed.

The room was darker.

And now he could see why.

The outer door, by which he had come in, was closed.

Jack went up and pushed it. It moved three centimetres or so, with a rattle, and then stopped. He pushed harder. But it was firm.

He thought of the latch. And realised, with a sinking heart, what had happened.

Someone had come along and put the padlock on.

They had locked up the works department.

And they had locked him in.

With two dead bodies under a dustsheet (OK, with a lathe and a grinder under a dustsheet, but it was still not good).

Jack looked around his prison.

There was the window, but, when he went over to examine it, he found it locked and barred. Well-locked, and well-barred.

He could try putting his shoulder to the door, but that would mean damaging the lock. He didn't want to do that.

Jack got out his mobile phone. The credit was low.

First he tried his mum's mobile, but that was switched off. He tried her office number, but after a few rings it went onto her answerphone.

Jack hit 'End Call' hard, then considered. He would have to ring the main number for Luke's. There was only one problem – he didn't have it.

He thought.

Marco. Marco could look it up for him. He rang Marco's mobile.

Marco answered promptly. "Hello, Jack!"

There was a noise like someone making an announcement over a tannoy.

"Hey, where are you?" said Jack.

"I'm at a bus and coach museum! It's great!"

"Oh," said Jack.

"There's uniforms and tickets and all sorts!" said Marco.

"Oh," said Jack.

"What do you want?"

"Erm...talk to you later!" Jack rang off.

He remembered an ad he had seen for a number finding service.

"What name, please?" said the man.

"St Luke's College, Oxford."

"Saint Luke's..."

There was silence.

Jack began to worry about his credit

"Saint..." said the man slowly. "See also Saints listed after "S...T..." He seemed to be reading from a screen.

"Please hurry!" said Jack.

"S...T..." said the man. "ST is listed after Saint..."

Jack bit his lip. Was the man spinning out the call on purpose? Or was he just thick?

Finally Jack got the number. But his credit was really low now.

It took some time for a porter to answer. And when he did, he could hardly hear what Jack was saying. There was a lot of shouting in the background.

"Sorry, what was that?" said the porter. "It's noisy here – there's a book being delivered."

Voices were arguing loudly.

"We'll have to open the gates!"

"No! Send it straight on!"

"We can't! It's too late!"

"Well, get the trailer back!"

"Typical rowers!"

"Why don't they *think*?"

It seemed a lot of bother for one book.

"OK," said the porter suddenly to Jack. "Say that again."

Jack drew a breath. "I'm lo—"

And then his credit gave out.

Jack put his mobile back in his pocket.

There was nothing for it. He got right up to the door.

"Er…excuse me!" he said in a normal voice.

No answer.

"Is anyone there?" Slightly louder.

No answer.

"*Hello!*" Louder still.

No answer.

"*CAN YOU HELP ME?*" Very loud.

No answer.

"HELP!"

His voice was hoarse before he got a response.

"Who's in there?" The voice came suddenly. It was a woman's voice, and it had a ring of authority.

"It's me!" said Jack. "I'm locked in!"

There was a pause.

"All right!" said the woman. "Don't panic! We'll be right back!"

He heard footsteps retreating.

Then silence. Quite a long silence. Then distant voices. The voices drawing closer. Then a scraping of a key in a padlock, then the louder scraping of the latch as it was pulled off its holder.

The door swung open, and Jack looked out.

Two people stood in front of him. Mr McGuffin, red-faced and annoyed, and a woman in a smart grey suit.

"I think we need an explanation, young man!" said the woman.

Joe looked back at her, not sure how to begin.

"I am the bursar of this college," she said. "And I repeat, I think we need an explanation!"

"Really, Jack!" said Mum. "You are the limit!"

Jack said nothing.

"Poor Mr McGuffin had only just got home!"

Carrie started whining.

"It's lucky the bursar's a friend!"

Carrie started whining louder.

"Mrs Bolton has enough to do without rescuing people from the works department!"

They were walking with Aunt Polly through Front Quad. A boat had suddenly appeared in the middle of the quad, but no one gave it a glance.

"I can't think what you were *doing*!" said Mum.

They stepped out of the college, and started walking to the bus stop. Jack watched the bikes go by. (Jack always watched bikes in Oxford now, but never saw *his* bike.)

Carrie put her arms up, and said, "Carry!" Mum carried her.

Suddenly Jack felt tired too.

"I mean, really, Jack!" said Mum. "If you'd only—"

"I did love the college!" said Aunt Polly. "I'd like to see more of Oxford!"

"Good idea!" said Mum. "Jack will show you!"

"Me?" said Jack. "I don't know anything about Oxford!"

"Then it's about time you learnt!" said Mum.

"There's a lot of it..." Jack said.

"Thirty-nine colleges!" said Mum brightly.

"Not all them are open to the public," said Aunt Polly.

Mum snorted. "And you can see why, can't you? When people start locking themselves into places!

I'm surprised *any* of them are open!"

"Thirty-nine colleges…" said Jack.

"Some of them are modern," said Aunt Polly.

Jack brightened. "You're not interested in modern buildings?"

"Modern architecture," said Aunt Polly, "is one of my great interests!"

"Oh."

They reached the bus stop. Mum put Carrie down.

A young woman pedalled past with a bunch of flowers in her rucksack

Jack stuck his hands in his pockets.

The day had not gone well…

12

A Closed Door

"Where," said Aunt Polly, "is the university?"

She looked up Broad Street.

She looked down Broad Street.

"Um…" said Jack.

"*Ha-hah!*" said Aunt Polly. "Trick question!" She read from her guide-book. "There's *no* university!"

"No," said Jack "There's definitely a university in Oxford."

Aunt Polly frowned. "Maybe I read that wrong." She looked in the book again. "Ah! There is no university *campus*, that's what I meant – it's more a collection of colleges." She waved the book around. "The university is all around us."

The Broad was busy. Tourists milled about. Students dodged through them. A smiling family were taking photographs of each other.

Jack looked around for something he could identify.

"Those are the Caesars!" He pointed to a row of huge stone heads. Aunt Polly riffled through her book.

"Ah, yes..." She read a few words. "Although here they're called the Emperors. Or the Bearded Ones."

Jack frowned. Just about the only thing he knew about Oxford University – apart from the fact that it existed – was being challenged. "No," he insisted. "They are definitely the Caesars. No one ever calls them the Bearded Ones."

Just then Aunt Polly, fumbling with her glasses, dropped her guidebook, which spun away across the pavement. A tall, elegant man in a bow tie stooped, picked it up, and presented it to her.

"Oh, thank you!" said Aunt Polly, taking the book. "Do tell me," she added. "What do you call those...er, heads?"

The tall man looked at the stone heads, then back at Aunt Polly. "It is one of my rules," he said in measured tones, "*nevah* to refer to them."

"Oh!" said Aunt Polly faintly.

With a slight nod of the head – not an unfriendly one – the tall man sped on.

"Gosh!" said Aunt Polly, deeply impressed. "I'm

sure he's a famous Oxford professor or something!"
She looked after his retreating figure. "I wonder what
his other rules are?"

But Jack was too busy to reply, avoiding someone
pushing a buggy.

"Right!" said Aunt Polly, looking at her guidebook
again. "So which is the Sheldonian, Jack?"

"Um…"

"Right here!" Aunt Polly nodded at the building in
front of them. "We are looking at its apse."

They looked at the apse, which was curved, and
then walked around and looked at the back, which
was flat.

Now they were in a paved space between three,
if not four, buildings. Suddenly it was much
quieter – a change after the crowds of Broad Street.

"That is the wall of…" Aunt Polly turned her book
sideways and squinted at a map. "The Divinity
School, I think."

Jack looked at the wall.

It was a fine wall.

The sort of wall any university would be proud of.

And it had a fine carved doorway, with a fine
wooden door in it. A closed door.

Jack wandered into the porch, and looked up.

On the ceiling of the porch was a star.

On the star was a model of an open book.

And on the model of the open book were some words.

Jack narrowed his eyes and tried read to them.

He failed. He could not read the words. He could not even read the letters. He frowned. He'd seen something like those letters not long before…

Aunt Polly joined him. "What are you looking at?" She followed his gaze. "Oh, look! A book!"

"Yes," said Jack. "But I can't make out the writing."

"No," said Aunt Polly. "Nor can I." She looked at her guidebook. "Nothing here."

"It's not Latin," said Jack. "If you can't read it, it's usually Latin. But this isn't."

"Well, let's find out!" And before Jack could stop her, Aunt Polly called out to a man walking past. "Excuse me?"

The man turned, eyebrows raised.

It was Professor Baker.

"Er…yes?" The professor shot Jack a slightly puzzled look as if he couldn't place him.

Aunt Polly gave a wide smile. "You don't happen to know about these letters up here?"

"Er, yes! Yes!" Professor Baker took a few steps towards them, and glanced up at the porch ceiling. "They are Greek."

"Greek?" said Jack in surprise. "Why Greek?"

There was a pause.

Andrew Baker looked at the pair in front of him.

He was already five minutes late for his meeting.

The scruffy boy and the woman with dyed-red hair did not look promising pupils.

But Andrew Baker loved his subject. More than he loved going to meetings.

He had been asked a question about his subject by someone who really wanted to know.

And when Andrew Baker was asked a question about his subject by someone who really wanted to know...

13

'In the Midst of The Teachers'

"It's a bit of Luke," said Professor Baker.

"*Luke?*" said Jack.

"The gospel according to St Luke."

Aunt Polly nodded. "The Bible."

"Indeed," said Professor Baker.

"But why," said Jack, "is it in Greek?"

"Because that's what Luke wrote it in."

"Oh."

"It means…" He glanced up. "They found him in the midst of the teachers."

"I know that bit!" cried Aunt Polly. "It's when his parents lose Jesus, then find him in the temple, surrounded by teachers!"

Professor Baker smiled at her. "Exactly."

"What a wonderful thing to have on a university

building!" cried Aunt Polly. "Don't you think, Jack?"

"Um..." Jack did not exactly warm to the idea of being "surrounded by teachers".

Professor Baker glanced at his watch. "And now I must—"

He was going. It was now or never.

"Professor Baker?" said Jack.

The professor looked at him.

"Those letters painted in the Luke's cloisters?" said Jack. "Were they Greek too?"

Professor Baker gave a start. "Yes! Yes, they were."

"From the Bible as well?"

"Yes."

"From St Luke?"

"No."

Jack persisted. "From what, then?"

"From...the Book of Revelation. Most likely, anyway." He turned on his heel.

"But what do they *mean?*" said Jack.

Professor Baker called back over his shoulder. "Six hundred, and sixty-six!" With that he was gone.

There was no doubt about it.

Aunt Polly was a generous aunt.

She ordered Jack a large Coke, and the second most expensive pizza on the menu.

Suddenly Jack was feeling better.

Sitting in the restaurant, swirling ice and lemon round with his black straw, he felt more cheerful than he had for days. Yes, his bike had been stolen, but maybe it was not the end of the world.

"It's about the end of the world," said Aunt Polly.

"What?"

"The Book of Revelation."

"Oh! You mean that book Professor Baker was talking about?"

"Yes. It's supposed to be about the end of the world."

"A bit depressing, then?"

"You could say that. It's full of death and disaster and weird animals. And the Whore of Babylon."

The waitress bringing their salads glanced at her sharply.

"Who's the Whore of Babylon?" said Jack.

"Not a nice girl, I imagine," said Aunt Polly.

There was silence.

Jack drank his Coke. "Professor Baker said the red letters meant a number. Six hundred and... something."

"Six hundred and sixty six," said Aunt Polly.

"Weird or what?"

Aunt Polly did not answer.

"I mean, why six hundred and sixty-six?"

Aunt Polly looked at him. "It's supposed to be evil."

14

Up The Tower

Jack stared at Aunt Polly. "*What?*"

Aunt Polly sipped her wine. "Six hundred and sixty-six is supposed to be an evil number."

"But why?"

"I don't know."

"An evil number…" Jack took a bit of carrot from his salad. "No wonder the professor looked like that when he saw it in the cloisters."

"Like what?" said Aunt Polly.

"Well…put out. No, *more* than put out." Jack thought. "He stared at it as if he couldn't quite believe his eyes."

The pizzas arrived.

Jack ate all his pizza, even the crust. Aunt Polly ordered him a second Coke, then handed him the dessert menu, saying, "Have what you like, Jack!"

Jack had what he liked. It was a sundae. It was ice cream with whipped cream and raspberry sauce and chocolate flakes and multi-coloured sprinkles.

As he was finishing, he started looking round at the other people. They were mostly shoppers, but at the next table were two men in crumpled jackets. They looked like dons.

Suddenly he was aware that Aunt Polly was talking.

"Apparently it's a good view from the top," she said.

He looked at her. "What?"

"And it's a nice day."

"What?"

"The tower!" Aunt Polly nodded towards Cornmarket. "I'm talking about climbing the tower!"

"What? Us?"

"Yes!"

He stared at her. "Aren't you a bit old for climbing towers?"

The next moment he felt a sharp blow to the side of his head.

He was under attack!

Who was it?

Who was hitting him?

Suddenly he realised.

It was Aunt Polly.

She had hit him on the head with her guidebook.

The two dons at the next table looked over with disapproval. They clearly thought that was *not* the way to treat books.

"What did you do that for?" he said, rubbing his head.

"Sorry!" said Aunt Polly. "I just meant to give you a playful tap."

"*A playful tap?*"

"Yes."

"But why hit me at all?"

"You suggested I'm too old to climb towers."

"Oh."

"And I'm not."

"No." Jack rubbed his head again.

"So we're going to climb the tower!"

"OK."

Aunt Polly smiled, and brought something out of her handbag. "And try these!"

"Binoculars!"

Aunt Polly nodded. "Neat, aren't they? I bought them yesterday!"

"St Michael's Tower is the oldest building in Oxford." Aunt Polly pushed open the door to the entrance, reading her book. "It was built as a lookout against the Danes."

They bought their tickets, and started their climb.

At first Jack leapt briskly up the wooden steps. But after a bit he began to feel rather sick. His sundae had been very rich. And very large. Jack put his hand to the wall. He'd better not let on to Aunt Polly, particularly after his remarks about her age. He could hear her climbing up behind him with steady steps. He kept on going.

Two-thirds of the way up, they found an old door with a notice on it. Five hundred years ago it had been a prison door. It had held the Oxford Martyrs, Cranmer, Latimer and Ridley, before they were burnt at the stake.

"Burnt for their religion!" Aunt Polly ran her hand over the dark wood. "Poor things!"

"Mm," said Jack.

"What a blot on Oxford's history!"

"Hey!" Jack's city was being criticised! He tried to remember what he had learnt at school. "They were *made* to burn them by Mary! Bloody Mary! She was Queen!"

Aunt Polly tutted. "Couldn't they say they'd *lost* them or something?"

They climbed on.

Soon they were nearing the top. The light grew in front of them.

They came out onto a surprisingly small square roof. A young couple were standing at one corner, but otherwise the roof was empty.

"Wow!" Aunt Polly looked around, panting slightly. "What a view!"

"Yeah!" said Jack. "The jeans shop has got a sale on!"

They looked down over Cornmarket, which was full of shoppers. The smell of burgers rose towards him. So did the strains of a fiddle played by a busker.

"We should be looking out for Danes!" said Aunt Polly. "Ah, spotted one!" She pointed at a tall blonde girl, wearing a rucksack.

"How do you know?" said Jack.

"Oh, I can spot a Dane a mile off!" Aunt Polly took in the view for a moment, then turned to Jack "This is great, isn't it?"

"It's OK," said Jack.

"It's better than OK!" said Aunt Polly. "Come on, Jack. Imagine you're a young Saxon on look-out!"

Jack gazed south towards Christ Church.

"Not that way!" cried Aunt Polly. "You'll get us all murdered! This is the north gate. Look north!"

Jack looked north.

"Right." Aunt Polly lowered her voice. "Now imagine you see something *move* out there."

Jack narrowed his eyes.

"You've *seen* something," said Aunt Polly. "And

you're not quite sure *what* you've seen. How scary is that?"

Jack nodded. "Yeah…"

Aunt Polly was thrilled with her binoculars. "Everything's bigger!" she cried, looking through them. "And closer!"

"Yes." Jack glanced around – he was rather glad the young couple had gone down.

"You can see so much more! Like those statues! And the pigeons! And…weird things!"

As he waited, Jack leant on the western railing, overlooking Cornmarket. He gazed down at St Michael's Street. It was much quieter than the other roads. In fact he could only see one person, a man walking on the pavement between a brick wall and a row of parked cars.

Suddenly it happened.

The man picked up a bike that was leaning against the wall. He carried it a few yards to a parked van, opened a back door, and swung it in. Slamming the door, he slipped round to the passenger door, opened it and got in. At once the van moved off.

It took seconds.

Jack had seen it.

But he was not quite sure what he had seen…

15

Kate

Jack gazed at the van.

Was he watching a bike being stolen? In the city centre? In broad daylight? His mind was racing. What should he do? He could not run down the tower. He would be sure to break a leg, and, anyway, it would be far too late to do anything. Number plate? No way at that distance! Jack peered desperately down into the street. The van was just about to turn the corner. If only—

"Binoculars! Quick!"

"Here!" Aunt Polly held them out.

Jack snatched the binoculars, and trained them on the van. But it was out of sight behind a building now. He ran a few steps towards the southwest corner, and the van came into view again. Desperately he twiddled the focus. An image sprang into his head, just as the van turned the corner.

"Hang them round the neck!" said Aunt Polly.

"*What?*"

"Hang them round your neck!" Aunt Polly pointed at the binoculars. "It's safer!"

Jack lowered the binoculars with shaking hands. "I've just seen a bike being stolen."

"Really?" Aunt Polly looked at him. "I wondered why you were so abrupt. Are you sure?"

Jack explained what he had seen.

"Hmm." Aunt Polly frowned. "It is quite a public place down there. Maybe they were just picking the bike up for some reason."

"It's possible." Jack gazed down into the street. Perhaps he had bike-stealing on the brain…

"So did you get the registration number?"

Jack frowned. *Did he get the registration number?* "Um…no. I thought I did. But I didn't."

"Oh, well." His aunt glanced at her watch. "Do you mind if we go to the Covered Market now? I'd like to buy your mum some fruit and stuff."

"Oh. OK." Jack glanced down at St Michael's Street. The van was long gone, and all seemed quiet. No one was shouting that their bike had gone. He turned, and followed Aunt Polly to the little entrance door. His heart had stopped beating quite so fast now…

"Kumquat!" cried Aunt Polly.

"Er...what?" said Jack.

"They've got kumquats!" Aunt Polly pointed to a display of fruit on the stall. "Let's get some! And some kiwi fruits! There's nothing like a kiwi!"

She bought some grapes too, and fresh dates, and some dried figs in dusty white sugar. "Isn't this fun!" said Aunt Polly.

When they had finished at the fruit stall, they strolled off. They admired the fish, but did not buy any. Then Aunt Polly said she wanted to get some cheese.

"Which cheese?" asked Jack.

"You know, the flat one."

"It was only flat because I fell on it."

"Yes, but what was it called?"

Jack was not likely to forget again. "Oxford Blue."

"Come on, let's go and get some."

They went up to the cheese stall. There was a man serving a customer, and they waited for him to finish. But then someone came from behind a big fridge, and said, "*Hey!*"

It was the girl.

"Hey!" said Jack. It was a bit feeble, but he couldn't think of anything else.

"Did you get your bike back?" said the girl.

Jack shook his head. "No! Not yet."

"Well, don't give up hope," said the girl.

"No," said Jack.

"You could look on the internet."

"Yeah," said Jack. "I'm doing that."

Aunt Polly asked for some Oxford Blue, and the girl reached over and picked up the wedge.

"Talking of stolen bikes," Jack said. "I think I've just seen one being stolen."

"Really?" The girl looked interested. "Where?"

"St Michael's Street."

The girl's mouth fell open. "*St Michael's Street?*"

"Yes!"

"I left *my* bike in St Michael's Street!"

"Well, it may not have been yours!" said Jack hastily. "And it may not have been stolen at all."

"So what did you see?"

"Well, this guy just threw a bike into the back of a van and drove off."

The girl frowned, and dropped the wedge of Oxford Blue. "I must check!" She turned to the man serving at the other end of the counter. "Ed, can I go for a minute?"

"OK, Kate," said Ed. "Be quick, though!"

Kate ran round in front of the counter. "Come on!" she said to Jack.

They charged down Cornmarket. It was crowded, and they swerved to avoid mums pushing buggies, a couple arm-in-arm, and a man wheeling a bicycle.

"Jack!" called a voice suddenly. "Jack!"

Suddenly he saw Marco barring his way. "What are you *doing*, Jack?"

Jack's heart sank. Marco glanced from him to Kate, and back again.

"Sorry, Marco!" Jack cried. "Got to go!"

"But—"

"Explain later!" And Jack jinked past Marco, and ran on.

"*Jack!*" he heard Marco calling after them.

They turned into St Michael's Street. Kate ran towards a cycle stand, which was full of bikes. "I can see it!" She reached the stand, and sort of patted one of the bikes.

Jack followed. "It's not even where I saw the bike taken from." He nodded towards the wall. "It was leaning against there."

"Even so, I'm going to move it!" Kate got out her keys, and started undoing the lock.

She pulled the bike from the stand, then paused and smiled at him. She had a nice smile. "Thanks, anyway."

He shrugged. "That's OK."

She gave a little frown. "A van, did you say?"

"Yes."

"What sort of van?"

"Er…white."

"Did you get the registration?"

He looked at her. Over her shoulder was a doorway. Something fluttered in Jack's mind, but he couldn't pin it down. "I thought I did, but I didn't."

"OK. What *make*?"

"Erm…"

"Ford Transit?" said Kate. "Toyota?"

"I don't know." Suddenly Jack felt depressed. Here was a girl about his age, who could not only sell cheese, but also knew about makes of van.

And while he no longer had a bike, she did.

He watched her wheel it away up the street.

Just before she turned the corner, she looked back and gave him another smile.

Yes, she definitely had a nice smile.

As Jack turned to go, he glanced up at St Michael's Tower.

It had gone.

A tower that had stood on the same spot for nearly a thousand years was gone.

Jack took a few steps down St Michael's Street.

The tower reappeared.

What was more, someone was standing at the top.

He – or she – stood absolutely still, looking north.

It was exactly the same spot Jack had stood less than an hour before.

Jack blinked and looked again.

He was mistaken.

There was no one there.

16

'Just a Number'

"But who is she?"

"I don't know! I don't know who she is!"

It was breaktime. Jack and Marco stood by the sports hall wall. They usually stood by the sports hall wall.

"You *must* know if you were running through Cornmarket with her," said Marco. "You don't run through Cornmarket with people you don't know."

Jack sighed. "Look, Marco, she...well, she sells cheese."

"She looks quite young to sell cheese, " said Marco.

"I think it's just a part-time job," said Jack.

"But why were you running through Cornmarket with her?"

Jack sighed again. "It's to do with my stolen bike."

"Did she steal your bike?"

"No."

"Does she *know* who stole your bike?"

"No."

There was silence. "I feel like some crisps," said Marco.

"OK," said Jack.

They walked towards the vending machines together.

"Marco?" said Jack.

"Yes?"

"Six hundred and sixty-six."

"What?"

"Six hundred and sixty-six."

"What?"

"Does six hundred and sixty-six mean anything to you?"

"No."

There were several people at the vending machine, so they had to wait.

"Are you sure?"

"Six hundred and sixty-six…" Marco frowned. "Well, it's definitely not a prime number."

Jack sighed. Marco did *mean* to be helpful.

"Hang on!" said Marco.

"What?" said Jack

"Did you say six, six, six?"

"Yes," said Jack.

"I've *seen* it! Here!"

"Where?"

"Carved on a tree!"

"Where?"

Marco nodded towards the sports field. "Just over there!"

"Come on then!" Jack shoved his money back into his pocket. "Show me!"

"All right!"

They were halfway across the sports field when the bell went.

"And I haven't even got my crisps," said Marco.

"Here it is!" Marco pointed proudly to the little tree. "Six hundred and sixty-six." And it was.

Someone had carved '666' into the silvery bark at about chest level. Probably with the point of a compass or something. Here and there the hand had slipped.

"But who did it?" said Jack.

"I don't know," said Marco. "I just saw it when it was done. I didn't see anyone do it."

Jack looked at the carving. "Did you know that six six six is supposed to be an evil number?"

"No," said Marco.

"Well, it is."

They gazed upon the number.

"Do you feel a sense of evil, Marco?"

"Well, I am feeling a bit peculiar," said Marco.

There was a laugh. They turned to see Hannah Jones. "A bit peculiar, did you say, Marco?" she said.

"Well, it's the numbers!" said Marco.

"What numbers?" said Hannah.

"*Those* numbers!"

Hannah looked at the numbers carved on the tree, and her expression changed. Not to one of horror. Just one of mild interest. "Six, six, six..." she murmured.

"It's supposed to be an evil number," said Jack.

"What nonsense!" said Hannah. "A number can't be evil! It's just a number!"

"It's in the Bible," said Jack.

"Maybe this is the tree of evil," said Marco.

"*Right.*" Hannah felt in her bag, and drew out a biro. With this she scratched a '1' before the first '6'. "There you are!" she said. "1666 – date of the Great Fire of London! It's not a tree of evil any more. It's a tree of history!"

A furious bark behind them made them all jump. "Stop that at once!"

They turned to see Mr Banerjee.

Mr Banerjee gave them a lecture about graffiti. And about a tree "needing its bark". Jack couldn't help thinking Mr Banerjee did *not* need *his* bark.

When he got his breath, Hannah told him she had only added the '1'.

"Oh, so it's this 'six, six, six' business again!" said Mr Banerjee.

"Again?" said Jack.

"Yes, I had to talk to Lindsay about it last week!" Then someone called him, and he was gone.

"Lindsay?" said Marco. "Who's Lindsay?"

Jack and Hannah looked at each other.

"Isn't she the Goth?" said Jack.

Hannah nodded. "Yup. Lindsay is the school Goth…"

Jack looked at Marco. "We'd better go and find her."

"Well, good luck!" said Hannah.

They started their search by walking towards the science block.

"We're looking," said Jack, "for someone wearing black."

Marco pointed across the playground to where Mr Andrews, the Head, was standing. He was wearing a dark suit. "What about him? Would *he* do?"

"Marco?"

"What?"

"Do you *want* to do this?"

"Oh, yes!" said Marco. "Hunting for Goths is just what I want to do in my spare time!"

They found Lindsay leaning on a low wall by the dining hall. Her clothes were black and torn, and held together with safety pins. Round her neck she wore a black leather collar with silver studs.

OK, thought Jack. He walked up to her. Marco followed a step or so behind.

"Er…Lindsay?" said Jack.

She turned her white face to them. "Yuh? What do you want?" The tone was not unfriendly.

"I just want to ask you about…well, the six six six you carved on the tree."

Her black-ringed eyes narrowed. "Yeah? Got a problem with it?"

"No, no!" said Jack hastily. "I just want to know, why six, six, six?"

Lindsay looked at him for a moment, then lowered her voice "It's the Number of the Beast."

Jack looked at Marco.

Marco gave his head a little shake.

Jack lowered his voice too. "What Beast?"

Lindsay frowned. "The devil."

"The devil?" said Jack. "Why the devil?"

"It just is, that's all!" Lindsay's voice was back to normal now.

"Is it?"

A dangerous note crept into her voice. "Maybe it's not a good idea to ask questions…"

Jack glanced at Marco. Not a good idea to ask questions? He was always asking questions, and so, for that matter, was Marco.

They turned to go.

"It's annoying, though," said Lindsay.

They turned back. Lindsay's hands, with black-painted nails, were playing lightly with her compass. There was a thoughtful look on her face.

Jack and Marco's eyes met.

"Er…what's annoying?"

"It's very difficult to carve, six six six. All those curves." She frowned. "Seven seven seven would be so much easier!"

17

The White Van

Jack stepped into St Luke's College. He glanced into the porter's lodge. Maybe Bill was in there? He could do with a friendly face.

There was someone in a porter's uniform, sitting at a desk by the CCTV monitors. He was looking at a big diary or something. Was it Bill?

Jack walked into the lodge. The porter looked up and smiled. It was Bill.

"Hi, Jack?" he said. "What are you after?"

"I'm looking for Mr McGuffin."

Bill jerked his head into the college. "He's around!"

There was silence.

"I've got to say sorry for something," said Jack.

"A-ha." Bill started writing something in the diary. Jack turned to go.

"I've found a new lake," said Bill.

Jack stopped in his tracks. "Have you?"

"It's good."

"Really?"

"Got some big'uns."

"Really?"

There was silence.

Bill turned a page of the diary. "I'll give you a ring."

The head of works was not difficult to find. Jack caught up with him at the little tree court. Mr McGuffin was walking towards the car park, carrying a large tool-box.

"Mr McGuffin?"

Mr McGuffin turned. "Yes?"

"I've come to say sorry."

"What?"

Jack drew a breath. "I'm sorry about getting locked in the works department. I shouldn't have been there. I was trying to be helpful, but I wasn't."

Phew!

Mr McGuffin put down his tool box, and surveyed him under bushy eyebrows. "I'd just boiled my kettle when I got that call."

"Yes. I'm sorry."

"You shouldn't step one *foot* in the works department!"

"No," said Jack.

"It's got machines, tools, paint-stripper – all sorts!"

"Yes," said Jack.

"Suppose you'd been injured…" Mr McGuffin shook his head.

"I know," said Jack.

"If I had my way the public wouldn't be let in to the college," said Mr McGuffin.

"No," said Jack. He didn't point out that he was not exactly public.

A wistful look came into Mr McGuffin's eye. "I'd put up a machine selling postcards by the porters' lodge, and that'd be as far as they could get."

"Yes," said Jack.

Mr McGuffin sighed. "But the fellows won't hear of it."

Jack looked at the tool box on the ground. There was a streak of red paint down the side.

"Mr McGuffin?"

"Yes?"

"About those red letters in the cloisters…"

"Terrible that."

"Who do you think did it?"

Jack was not really expecting an answer. But Mr McGuffin seemed quite willing to talk about the outrage to his cloisters. He shook his head. "Such a pity it was that corner."

"Why?"

"It's just out of range of the CCTV cameras."

"Oh."

"Between you and me, I blame the bursar."

"The *bursar* did it?"

"No, no!" said Mr McGuffin. "I wanted a CCTV upgrade, but Mrs Bolton wouldn't have it."

"Oh."

"She spent the money on drains."

"Oh."

A glimmer of satisfaction passed over Mr McGuffin's face. "She'll have to agree to it now, though. After this!"

Jack looked at him. "Do you think a Luke's person did it?"

"Hard to be certain," said the head of works. "But I think so. It was done after midnight, when the gates are closed. The Dean, Eric Marshall, walked past at about twenty past and he was sure the wall was clear then."

"So who *is* in college at night?" asked Jack.

"Well, the students, of course. And the Master. And a few fellows. The Dean, for one."

"What about...Cecil and Alfred?"

"No, no, they're long retired. They don't have rooms in college." Mr McGuffin was thoughtful. "Some of the graduates have rooms, though.

Like that David Bradshaw."

"David Bradshaw?"

"Pale chap. Theology, I think he does. Religion, anyway!"

"I don't think I've met him," said Jack.

"Well, he spends a lot of time in the chapel." Mr McGuffin picked up his tool box. "And now I must get on. It's hard work, maintaining a college!"

"I'm sure!" said Jack. "Would you like some help?"

To his surprise, the head of works nodded. "I wouldn't mind a hand with mending a slat in the car park," he said.

"OK!" said Jack.

"But you're not to sue if I hit your finger with a hammer."

"I won't!" said Jack.

The two of them set off down the path.

The small car park was just about full, as usual. The cars ranged from an old BMW to a new Mini.

Between them the slat in the fence was quickly mended. "That'll hold it for now," said Mr McGuffin. He scratched his head, and surveyed the length of the fence. "We'll have to replace it soon, though."

Someone drove into the car park, and, after some manoeuvring, managed to fit into a space.

The driver got out, locked the driver's door, and set out up the path.

"That's Professor Baker," said Mr McGuffin, looking after him. "Probably back from Cambridge or somewhere. Always in demand, our Professor Baker."

Jack stood stock-still.

He stared at the professor's vehicle.

It was a white van.

18

Il capo?

Mr McGuffin closed his tool box with a click. "Best be getting on now."

Jack's mind was racing. A white van! Was it *the* white van? The one he had seen taking the bike in St Michael's Street? It was certainly very like it!

And surely it was the van that once nearly knocked him over!

"Come on!" Mr McGuffin led the way up the path.

Jack followed him. There was not much else he could do.

They parted at the little tree court. "You be finding your mum, now," said Mr McGuffin, turning left

"OK," said Jack. "Bye, Mr McGuffin!"

As soon as Mr McGuffin was out of sight, Jack

leant back against a wall. He had to think this one through…

Was Professor Baker a bicycle thief? Surely not, a professor of classics at Oxford University! But what a superb cover! All those trips he took to Cambridge and London and places! He could be taking bikes to sell there, and nicking new ones! It was *brilliant!* There was another thing too – why ever would a classics professor drive a white van?

But Professor Baker was definitely not the man he'd seen taking the bike in St Michael's Street. That man was younger and shorter. So perhaps Professor Baker was the head of a gang? What was that Italian phrase Marco used? *Il capo*. That was it. The head. Or maybe Professor Baker was *il capo di tutti capi*. The head of all heads?

Suddenly Jack wished Marco was there.

But Jack was on his own.

And he knew what he had to do.

Now.

He turned back the way he had come.

As he walked into the car park, Jack looked around. He was in luck. The car park was deserted. He crept up to the passenger door of the white van, and looked in through the window. There was not much to see; just a map and a plastic bag on the passenger seat. It all looked very ordinary.

Jack peered round behind, but there was a partition so he couldn't see into the back. But that was where everything would be. The stolen bikes. The wire-cutters. The files...

He sidled round to the back of the van. But there were no windows there. What could he do now? Nothing, that was what. Absolutely nothing. Unless, of course, the back door was unlocked.

Jack had seen Professor Baker lock the driver's door. The van probably had central locking.

But it was just worth a try.

He reached out for the handle.

Pressed it down.

And it opened.

"Wow!" thought Jack. Heart in his mouth, he pulled the door back, and looked in.

There were no bicycles in the van.

There were not even bits of bicycles.

Or wire-cutters.

Or files.

Well, there *were* files. But not the sort of files you file metal with. They were the sort of files you file papers in.

Jack frowned.

Suddenly he heard a loud voice. "*What* do you think you're doing?"

He turned to see someone striding across the car park.

It was the professor.

And the professor looked angry.

It was a nasty moment. Jack wondered whether to run.

After all, he might be alone in Luke's car-park with a dangerous bicycle thief who might bundle Jack into the van, and...get *rid* of him.

But somehow Professor Baker didn't *look* like a dangerous bicycle thief. He looked more like an angry classics professor.

Jack did not run.

Professor Baker reached the van. "What are you *doing*?" he repeated.

Jack looked at him. "I was looking for something."

"Looking for something? *What?*"

"I was looking for..." And then Jack had an inspiration. "A Bible!"

19
Looking for a Bible

"A *Bible?*" The professor stared at him.

"Yes," said Jack. "I need a Bible."

"But you can't go poking around in vans looking for Bibles!"

"No," said Jack.

"Hang on!" Professor Baker looked in his face. "You're Mrs Young's boy, aren't you?"

Jack nodded glumly. Coming to Luke's to say sorry had been a failure. He'd gone and got into even more trouble.

The professor was silent for a moment, then said, "Right!" He took a blue file out of the back of the van, locked all the doors, then turned to Jack.

"Come on!" he said. "I'm teaching in a minute, but you can explain as we go!"

They started up the path. "Well?" said Professor Baker.

Joe took a breath. "I need a Bible to find out about those red letters in the cloisters."

"Oh, those!" said Professor Baker. "You shouldn't worry about those!"

"You said they meant six hundred and sixty-six. But how? And what does six hundred and sixty-six mean? No one will tell me!"

"Yes," said the professor. "It's annoying when that happens. *So...*" He put up a forefinger, and drew in the air. "Those letters are Greek – they're called *chi, xi, sigma*."

"Right," said Jack.

"They're ordinary letters, but they were also used as numbers. That's where you get the six six six. In chapter thirteen of Revelation, at the end of the Bible, six six six is said to be *the Number of the Beast*."

"And what does that mean?" said Jack.

"I'm not sure," said Professor Baker.

"*What?*" said Jack.

"I'm not sure."

"But you're a professor at Oxford!"

Professor Baker smiled. "Yes. And a professor at Oxford won't pretend he knows something he doesn't. Not usually, anyway." He looked sideways at Jack. "I've even written a book about Revelation."

"Have you?" said Jack.

"Yes. And I still don't know what *the Number of the Beast* means."

"Well, if you don't know," said Jack. "What hope is there for me?"

Professor Baker shrugged. "Who knows, you might have a brilliant idea!"

"But how…"

"Find a Bible, and have a look!" Professor Baker glanced at him. "Though, if I may say so, a white van is probably not the best place to look."

"No," said Jack.

"Even the Luke's van."

"The *Luke's* van?" said Jack.

"Yes," said Professor Baker. "The van belongs to St Luke's. The college has a house in Italy and I sometimes drive stuff out there. In return, they let me use it whenever I want."

They had now reached the little tree court. Two young women were walking by the tree. The blonde one, who looked familiar, shot a glance at the professor.

Jack thought. "Would you take it to London, then?"

"No," said the professor. "I never drive to London. I take the bus or train."

So it was *not* the professor who'd nearly knocked into him that day. Jack felt pleased about that.

They were now walking up the passage towards the cloisters. On the left was the high wall of the New Library. On the right, at intervals, were several doors. At the last door on the right, a student was waiting. He was clutching some books, and seemed anxious.

"Hello, Thomas!" Professor Baker called cheerily.

Thomas looked relieved. "Oh, it was this time!"

"Yes, yes!" said Professor Baker. "Come on in. Homer awaits!"

Homer? Jack looked at the professor with fresh interest.

Professor Baker unlocked his door, nodded at Jack, and he and Thomas disappeared into his room, talking about an essay.

Jack walked on.

He spent a few minutes looking at a notice board. It had all sorts of stuff. There was a poster for a '*Crazy Ox* disco', with a cartoon ox dancing on one hoof. There were several club notices, including a bright pink one for the Boat Club. There was a list of times people could see the Dean.

Maisie pattered by, and he had a quick word with her.

As he was tickling her under the chin, someone strolled past. Jack looked up to see Alex. He was surprised to see him turning into Professor Baker's room. If he was joining the tutorial, he was very late...

Jack went into the cloisters. He stood at one of the arches leading to the central lawn. He gazed round at the view – the view that had been painted and photographed and filmed so often.

There was the Hall, where everyone ate together.

Nearby was the Founder's Tower, which held the college archives.

Down that way was the Old Library.

And looming behind the cloisters was the chapel.

The chapel…

Chapels had Bibles in them.

Didn't they?

20

A Beast Arises

Jack could hear it even before he got to the antechapel door.

Someone was playing the organ.

It was probably the organ scholar, Jack thought.

He remembered Mum talking about organ scholars. St Luke's, she said, always got good organ scholars. Other colleges, it seemed, sometimes had organ scholars who were not so good. But Luke's ones always – as it were – pulled out the stops.

Jack felt a thrill of pride. Really, Luke's was a very fine college.

He opened the door to the antechapel, and walked in. There was no one to be seen. The organ music swelled and swooped, its rich sound rising to the rafters. Whoever was playing would be in the organ loft, up a flight of stairs.

Jack gazed around. There were several rows of chairs in the middle of the antechapel, and some tables by the side. Jack had a hunt round, but he could not find a Bible anywhere. There were some leaflets with prayers and stuff on, but no Bibles.

He went over to the bronze gates that led into the chapel itself. Normally these were locked, except for services. But, to his surprise, Jack saw that one of the gates was slightly ajar. He peered into the gloom. There didn't seem to be anyone there.

Jack slipped through the gates. He would only go in a few feet – just to see if he could spot a Bible…

There was no Bible in the raised wooden seats at the sides, and Jack was just about to go back to the antechapel, when he looked down the length of the nave.

There, two thirds of the way towards the altar, glowing in the gloom, was an eagle.

It was a golden eagle, and it stood on a gold stand, watching him with beady eyes. Behind its handsome head was a great open book. And Jack knew at once what that open book was.

Jack should not have gone up to the golden eagle. He knew that. He shouldn't have been in the chapel at all, let alone two-thirds of the way up it.

But the organ music rang in his ears.

The golden eagle challenged him.

And Professor Baker had *told* him to look at a Bible!

He walked slowly up to the stand, then swung round behind it, so his back was to the altar.

Then he looked at the open book.

It *was* the Bible, a magnificent volume that took up his whole view. The print was large, and even though the chapel was dark, Jack could read it easily. It was open at 'The Gospel according to Saint Luke'.

But where was the Book of Revelation?

Hadn't Professor Baker said it was at the end of the Bible?

Jack put his hand to the huge page, and turned it gingerly over. *Luke 3. Luke 4…*

He went on turning the pages. *Romans, Hebrews, Jude…*

The left-hand side of the great book got thicker and thicker.

The right hand side got thinner and thinner.

The spine shifted beneath his hands.

And then there it was.

The Book of Revelation.

Jack started reading. It was all very strange. It didn't seem to be about real people at all, but was full of angels and trumpets and monsters and warnings. And death. There seemed to be a lot of death.

The organ music, which had sounded happy and lively, now seemed full of doom. The chords crashed about his ears.

Chapter 13, that was what Professor Baker had said. Chapter 13...

When he found it, he read, *"Then I stood on the sand of the sea."*

That sounded OK.

But the next words were not. *"And I saw a beast rising out of the sea."*

There was something about those words that made his scalp prickle.

Jack was in a scary dark chapel, listening to scary loud music, reading a scary great book. It was not good. But he *had* to find out about the numbers. The black letters danced before his eyes. He made an effort to focus and read on. Another beast arose, this time from the earth.

And then he found it. *"Let him who has understanding calculate the number of the beast, for it is the number of a man: His number is 666."*

At that instant, the organ music stopped.

The chapel became even darker.

And from behind the Bible a beast arose.

21

David Bradshaw

Jack gasped in pure fear. He jumped back, and crouched down. The golden eagle was not much protection, but it was all he had.

He gazed up, heart hammering.

It was not a beast that had arisen before him.

It was a man.

A young man with a pale face.

And he did not look about to attack.

Jack stayed crouching for a second or two.

His heart was still thumping.

His blood was still pounding in his ears.

Then he slowly rose to his feet.

He looked into the pale man's face. He did not look angry, or even surprised. He just looked sad.

"What are you doing here?" said the man in a low voice.

Jack did not answer.

"What are you doing here?" repeated the man.

"I...I was reading the Bible," said Jack.

The man came round the stand, and looked at the page he was at. Without a word, he turned the pages back to Luke.

"You must go now," said the man. "I must lock up. I should have locked up before, and I must lock up now."

"Yes," said Jack.

The man took Jack down the chapel to the gates, and stood while Jack slipped through into the antechapel.

"I shall lock up now," he said.

"Right," said Jack. And then the man did something Jack didn't expect. He locked the gates with himself *inside*, then walked rapidly away in the direction of the altar.

Jack let out a breath, and looked about the antechapel. He could hear steps. Brisk steps. Someone was coming down the stairs from the organ loft.

Jack made brisk steps himself – for the door. He did not want to meet any more weird people.

He had nearly reached the door, when a voice rang out.

"*Excuse me?*"

Slowly Jack turned. Standing at the bottom of the organ loft stairs was a girl. She did not look weird. She looked all right.

"Yes?" he said.

"Did I hear you talking to David Bradshaw?"

"I don't know," said Jack. "I was talking to someone, but I don't know his name."

The girl came closer. "Sort of thin with dark hair?"

"Yes," said Jack. "That would be him. He's just locked up the chapel – in fact he's locked himself in."

The girl looked towards the chapel. "Oh, dear."

"It's OK," said Jack. "He should be quite safe in there."

"It's not that!" said the girl. "It's what is he *doing* in there all the time?"

Jack shrugged.

"He should be working on his thesis!" said the girl.

"Perhaps his thesis is on the inside of a chapel," said Jack.

"It's not!" said the girl. "It's on apocalyptical writing."

"What?" said Jack.

"Apocalyptical writing!"

Jack didn't know what that meant. He also knew it was much easier not to ask. "What's that?" he said.

"It's writing about…the Apocalypse, I suppose.

Mysteries, and the end of the world and things."

"Oh," said Jack. "Yes."

"David was doing so well and had all these theories." The girl glanced towards the chapel. "He's got a brilliant mind."

Jack nodded.

The girl lowered her voice, although the antechapel was quite empty. "And do you know what?"

"No," said Jack. "What?"

"Well, David talked about his theories to someone once, and…"

"Yes?" prompted Jack.

"He's gone and put David's ideas in his own book!"

"Hmm."

"It's terrible!" cried the girl. "As if someone pinched one of my compositions!" Her face darkened. And suddenly Jack saw she'd be quite an enemy to make…

22

A Revelation

Ker-plunk, ker-plunk, plunketty, plunk!

"Can I have a go?" asked Marco.

The pianist took no notice, but started on the next movement. *Ker-plunk, ker-plunk, plunketty!*

"Wouldn't you like to play with your phone?" Marco held the red plastic phone towards her.

"Nah!" said the pianist.

"Don't worry," said Jack. "She'll probably get bored of it soon."

"I *never* had a piano when I was little!" said Marco.

"Well, toy pianos aren't much good, really." Jack thought of the swelling chords of the Luke's organ.

"Has your Aunt Polly given *you* anything?" said Marco.

Jack thought. "No, but she's taking Mum and me

out to a restaurant tomorrow. It's supposed to be really good."

"Not Carrie?"

"No," said Jack. "She's too young."

Marco looked at the piano, and sighed

Ker-plunk, ker-plunk, plunketty, PLUNK.

The thin brush dipped into the red liquid. Then it was raised aloft, drops falling silently back into the reddy pool. Yes, there was plenty left. Plenty. It was time to get going again...

"My God!" Jack stared in horror.

"What, Jack?" said Aunt Polly.

"Look at these *prices!*"

Mum lowered her menu, and looked at him. "You shouldn't really talk about the prices when someone's treating you."

"Oh," said Jack.

Aunt Polly winked at him.

They were sitting at a pink table in the first floor restaurant. Their table was right by the window, and Jack had a good view. But right now he was not thinking about the view. He was thinking about food.

"Mmm, nice menu!" said Mum.

"I can't see chips," said Jack. "Are you sure they

have chips? They must have chips! What's the point of a restaurant without chips?"

"Calm down, Jack!" Mum pointed at the menu. "There you are – *pommes frites!*"

Jack calmed down.

"Oh, look!" said Aunt Polly. "Ox tail!"

"*Ox tail?*" said Jack. "The tail of an ox?"

"That's right," said Aunt Polly. "It can be delicious."

"Isn't it rather…hairy?"

Mum laughed. "It's not the hairy part! It's the muscle part!"

"Oh," said Jack.

"It says it's organic," said Aunt Polly. "I think I'll have it."

The waiter came up, and took their order. After that there was silence.

It was Jack who spoke first. "What *is* an ox exactly?"

Mum and Aunt Polly looked at each other

"It's a castrated bullock," said Aunt Polly.

"They cut the testicles off," said Mum.

"Oof!" said Jack.

"They grow huge," said Mum.

"What do?" said Jack.

"The oxen," said Mum.

"It makes them good for haulage and stuff," said Aunt Polly.

"And oxen aren't as bad-tempered as bulls," said Mum.

"Mind you," said Aunt Polly. "There aren't many oxen in the west any more."

"No," Mum nodded. "So ox tail just means beef tail, really."

Aunt Polly frowned. "Strange symbol for Saint Luke, though."

"It's a symbol of sacrifice," said Mum.

"Ah, yes," said Aunt Polly. "Sacrifice…"

Their starters arrived, and they started talking about the college. There was always something going on, Mum said.

"Like what?" said Aunt Polly.

Mum glanced around. There was no one sitting nearby, but even so she leant forward and lowered her voice. "There's an old lecture-hall the Master wants to demolish. He wants to use the site for student accommodation. But some of the fellows are up in arms."

"Professor Baker?" said Jack.

Mum looked at him. "He's one of the main people opposing the Master." She sipped her wine. "The whole thing's got very bitter. Someone has even been accused of hiding vital documents."

They also talked about the red letters. "It's not just the vandalism that's upset people," Mum said. "It's also the reference to the Bible."

"Hmm," said Aunt Polly. "You do get a better class of graffiti in Oxford."

Mum opened her mouth to say something, but just then the main courses arrived. Aunt Polly's ox tail turned out to be round rings of meat in a dark sauce, and looked quite nice. Mum had something with aubergines. Jack had steak and chips and salad. When he had eaten most of his steak, he started gazing out of the window.

The restaurant looked over a road, and, beyond the road was a pavement, half of which was a cycle lane. Though it was dark now, the area was well lit by street lamps. It was fun, sitting in the warm restaurant, watching people cycle home in the dusk.

Someone was biking slowly along, pulling a child in a covered wagon. One man was pedalling madly in a very low gear. The next person's bike lights were not working.

Suddenly a cyclist in black swooped up the bike lane. Jack watched as, nearly across from the restaurant, he or she braked to a stop, and got off. Then the cyclist leant the bike against the hedge, turned and walked off.

Jack cut some more steak.

"No more wine for me!" Mum was saying to the waiter. "I'm driving."

"Could we have some more water?" said Aunt Polly.

A moment later Jack glanced out of the window, chewing a bit of lettuce.

He saw something that made him start.

Someone in a bright yellow raincoat was standing by the hedge. Right by the bike that the cyclist in black had just left.

He was not just standing by the bike either.

He was pulling it out from the hedge, and then, before Jack's eyes, he leapt onto the bike, and rode off.

This time there was no doubt about it – Jack was seeing a bicycle being stolen!

As the rider in the yellow raincoat came into the pool of light by the next lamppost, Jack had a very good view of his face.

Though it was not *his* face.

It was *her* face.

Kate.

23

Chase through the Dark

Jack was stunned.

He sat there, holding a bit of lettuce.

Kate a bicycle thief! Surely not! But he had seen it! Seen *her!*

He did not want to believe it.

But he had to believe it.

He felt sick.

He shook his head when Aunt Polly asked if he wanted a pudding. She looked surprised, and turned to Mum.

"No thanks," said Mum. "But would you mind if we went to college on the way home?"

"Not at all!" said Aunt Polly.

"It's that lecture hall thing we were talking about," said Mum. "I've an awful feeling I didn't lock the file away properly." She sighed, and crumpled her napkin. "It's been worrying me."

Aunt Polly smiled. "Of course we can go back. I'll get the bill." And she waved at a waiter.

Choose the time carefully, that was the thing. When there was no-one about. Drip, drip, drip. The liquid was so red, so thick – lovely…

Mum put her key-card in the machine, and the gate swung open. The car park was dark and shadowy, with just one light by the entrance to the road, and one by the exit to the path. But there were several free spaces, and Mum eased the car into the nearest. "I won't be a minute," she said, opening her door.

"No hurry!" said Aunt Polly.

Jack sat back, and closed his eyes. He felt tired suddenly. A second or so later, he heard a gasp.

Jack sat up, and peered through his window. Only a few feet away, in the dark, Mum was staggering, arms waving.

He stared in horror. Someone – or something – was attacking his mother!

He opened the door to go to her rescue, but Mum had now reached the car, and was pulling her door open.

"Blast!" she said, swinging herself in. "Blast, blast, blast!"

"*What?*" said Jack.

Mum took a shoe off, and waved it around. "A broken heel!"

"How sad!" said Aunt Polly. "Such lovely shoes!"

"I thought you'd been hurt," said Jack in a low voice.

Mum leant back in her seat and groaned. "*Now what?*"

"Can't you walk at all?" said Aunt Polly.

"Not without people thinking I'm drunk or something!" said Mum. "That will look good, a secretary staggering around college at this hour of night!" She gave a short laugh. "Great example for the students!"

"But you're not drunk," said Aunt Polly.

"I know I'm not drunk!" said Mum a bit irritably. "But with my luck I'll bump into the Master with…the Education Minister or someone! They'll probably halve our funding because of me!"

"I don't think—"

"Jack!" Mum interrupted, turning round.

"Yes?"

"You'll have to go!"

"OK."

"And you'd better take Aunt Polly with you!"

"No need!" said Jack quickly "I'll be fine on my own!"

Mum looked at him for a moment, then said, "OK." She gave him a bunch of keys, and a load of instructions.

He got out of the car, and set off.

The path was better lit than the car park, and Jack sped up it. He passed three people, who were making for the car park, then sprinted through the tree court.

He walked along the wall of the New Library. The lights were still on, and he jumped in the air to look through the windows. Yup, people were working even this late! Several were sitting at tables, deep in their books. One of them was Thomas, Professor Baker's pupil. Probably hard at work on the Simpsons...

Jack went on to the cloisters. He had never been in them at night. They were lit well enough to walk along, but were still shadowy and mysterious. Just ahead of him, someone in a black gown whisked round the corner, tails flapping. He – or she – had probably been dining in formal hall.

He got to Mum's office without anyone challenging him. He looked at his bunch of keys. Now, what had Mum said...?

Ah, yes! He unlocked the first door, then the second, turning the key round twice. He slipped in, finding the light switches easily. The strip lighting came on in a series of flashes, lighting up the tidy office. Jack went over to Mum's desk, leant over her chair, and tried the top drawer on the right-hand side.

It was locked. Quite clearly locked. And there were no files at all lying around. So much for Mum's worrying.

Locking the doors carefully, he started back the way he had come. He heard a scuffle and a giggle from the other side of the cloisters, near the college bar. But there were not many people around.

His thoughts turned to the restaurant they'd just left. He was beginning to regret he had not had a pudding. There was a chocolaty thing on the menu which had looked interesting. Meringue in it somewhere. And nuts...?

He turned into the passage leading to the tree court.

Someone ahead was walking quickly away.

Jack suddenly felt alert.

A lot of people walked quickly through St Luke's College. The term time was very busy. But somehow this was different. It wasn't the walk of someone who was late. It was the walk of someone trying to get away.

Jack felt a prickle at the back of his neck. Perhaps he should just go back to the cloisters, and wait until someone else came down the passage.

No. He would go on.

Jack walked on down the passage.

His feet sounded on the concrete.

There was a slight breeze.

Aaaargh!

Jack stopped stock-still.

And nearly let out a shout.

There, on the door to his left, were three gleaming marks.

They looked nearly black in the dark, but Jack knew they were not black.

He knew they were blood-red.

He stared at them.

They were the same Greek letters that had been written before. *Chi, xi, sigma*. And Jack now knew what they meant.

They meant six hundred and sixty-six. The Number of the Beast.

There was something else. Jack knew whose door the letters were painted on. The door – and the room inside the door – belonged to Professor Baker.

Jack stepped nearer. Very slowly he put out a finger and touched the *chi* near the middle of the cross. It felt sticky. When he took his finger away, he could see a stain on it.

Suddenly something caught his eye. He turned his head, and looked down the passage to the tree court.

There was someone there.

Jack ran.

As he neared the court, the figure moved off to the right. Jack put on an extra spurt. He sped into the tree court, and rounded to the right. Ahead of him someone walked steadily away. Jack pelted after them. "Hey, you!" he cried. "Stop!"

The person turned, a look of surprise on his face.

Jack's mouth fell open.

It was Bill. His friend Bill, the porter.

24

A Mad Professor?

"How could you be so *stupid*?" said Marco.

They both looked at Jack's red fingertip.

"Leaving your prints on the paint! They'll think it was you!"

Jack shrugged.

Marco looked thoughtful. "You could always say it was a cry for help."

"*Marco*! I didn't do it!"

They were standing behind the sports hall. Not that many people used the path behind the sports hall.

"So who did, then?" Marco riffled his physics book.

"Well, not Bill."

"Why not Bill?"

"I know Bill from fishing."

"So?"

"You *know* someone if you fish with them."

Marco rolled his eyes.

They stopped talking as a senior girl came past.

Then Marco said, "But why were the letters painted on the *professor's* door? Just by chance?"

"I don't think so," said Jack. "Those letters in the cloisters, the first ones. They were right by the passage to his room."

"So they're getting closer."

Jack nodded. "Yes. And, of course, he can read the letters. He knows what they mean."

"But why target Professor Baker?"

"Well...maybe someone is jealous."

"Do you think?"

"Well, he's very successful," said Jack. "He's written lots of books. Mum said he was on telly the other day."

Some Year Sixes came panting along the path.

Then Marco said, "I know who it is!"

Jack looked at him. "Who?"

Marco gave a smile of triumph. "Professor Baker! He's doing it to himself!"

"Oh, yeah?" said Jack. "And why would he do that?"

"Because he's mad!" said Marco. "Aren't professors supposed to be mad?"

"No!" said Jack. "That's just telly! Professors aren't all wild-haired and stuff!" He thought. "Well, only when it's very windy."

There was silence.

Marco riffled his text-book again. "That evil number stuff is sort of scary..."

Jack nodded.

Marco narrowed his eyes. "You don't think it was written by something...inhuman?"

"Well, there's the college cat, but I don't think Maisie—"

"I mean something...*inhuman*."

"Well, there's the college cat, but I don't think Maisie—"

"I mean something INHUMAN!"

"*What*?" said Jack.

"Something...you know...*not of this world*!" Marco held the textbook over his face, and spoke in a whisper behind it. "Something beyond the laws of physics!"

Jack looked at the picture of the scales on the front of the book. "No."

Marco took his text-book down. "Why not?"

"It was blobby."

"*Blobby?*"

"The paint, or whatever it was, was blobby at the bottom. Nearly dribbling."

"So...?"

"*Gravity*, Marco."

"Jack—"

"And if the *writing* obeyed the laws of physics," said Jack. "I reckon the *writer* obeyed the laws of physics."

"Jack—"

"I think, my friend, we should be looking for a *rational* explanation."

Marco hit him on the head with the physics book.

Jack rubbed his head. "Why do people always hit me on the head with books?"

Marco leant against the sports hall wall, sticking his feet out. "So come on. Who do you reckon did it?"

"Well," said Jack. "I think it would be someone who can write Greek letters. They're different from English ones."

"Couldn't they just copy them?" Marco lowered his back, and stuck his feet out even further.

"Not really. I think you'd have to know how to do them. And, anyway, why would you bother? Why not write six six six like Lindsay?"

"Yes..." Marco looked up at him thoughtfully. "I see what you mean. So it would be someone doing Greek."

Jack nodded. "They're called classicists."

"Well, there can't be many of those!" said Marco. His feet were right out into the path now.

"There are lots of classicists in Oxford," said Jack. "More per acre than anywhere else in the world."

"Like New Zealand and sheep."

"No, that's different."

"It isn't!" said Marco.

"It is!" said Jack.

Someone walking along the path came to an abrupt stop. It was Hannah Jones. "I can't get past your great feet!" she said.

"They're not great feet," said Marco. "They're just stuck out a long way."

"Well, stick them back in!"

Marco gazed up at her from the wall. "I'm defying the laws of gravity."

"You're not!" cried Hannah. "You're nowhere *near* defying the laws of gravity! You're just in my way!"

"It helps me think, having stuck-out feet," said Marco.

"Well, it doesn't help me walk!" Hannah looked at him. "What are you thinking about, anyway?"

"Sheep," said Marco.

"Not evil numbers?"

"Those too," said Marco. "Sheep and evil numbers."

"I take it back!" said Hannah. "You need all the help you can get. If stuck-out feet help you think, carry on sticking!" And she stepped over

Marco's feet, and walked on.

"Girls!" said Marco, but he shuffled upright again. "Talking of girls," he said, "I've met your cheese girl."

"*What?*"

"I met your cheese girl!" said Marco happily. "There aren't *that* many cheese shops in Oxford. I told her she didn't have enough Italian cheese."

Jack stared at him in horror. "But—"

"She doesn't know that much about cheese, actually. I was quite surprised. She hadn't even *heard* of fontina, one of the best Itali—"

"She's a bicycle thief!" said Jack.

"What?" It was Marco's turn to stare. "But you said she wasn't!"

"I was wrong!" said Jack. "I saw her steal one with my own eyes!" And he told him what he'd seen from the restaurant.

"I don't believe it!" cried Marco. "She seemed so nice! Not very knowledgeable about cheese, but very nice!"

"I know," said Jack miserably.

Marco pursed his lips. "*When* did you say you first met her?"

"Just after I found my bike stolen."

"I bet she stole it herself!" cried Marco. "She stole it herself, and was revisiting the scene of the crime!"

"Don't get so carried *away*, Marco," said Jack.

"That's murderers."

Marco shrugged. "You should have rung the police."

"When?"

"After you saw her from the restaurant."

"Hmm."

"Why didn't you?"

"Well…" Jack took a deep breath. "It's not quite as simple as that."

"Why not?"

Why not? He couldn't really explain it himself. "I just…can't shop Kate."

"Well, if everyone thought like that, the police would never catch anybody!"

Some Year Twelves stalked by.

"I wish now I hadn't told her about St Luke's," said Marco.

This took a few seconds to sink in.

"*What* did you say?"

"I wish I hadn't told her about Luke's."

Jack stared at him. "You told her about *Luke's?*"

"Yes, your mum working there and stuff. She asked about you, and I told her."

Jack thumped a hand in his fist. "How could you, Marco?"

"I didn't *know* she was a bicycle thief," said Marco. "Otherwise I'd have said Christ Church."

"Christ Church? Why Christ Church?"

"It's the only one I've heard of apart from Luke's."

There was a long silence.

Then the bell went. Marco picked his physics book up from the ground. "White spirit," he said.

"What?" said Jack.

"White spirit. It's the best thing for getting paint off."

They both looked at Jack's red fingertip.

25

Friars of Doom

Time to make a move again. Something a bit different this time. Better be careful, though. Last time someone nearly caught you. Carefully does it, that's the way…

Jack went to Marco's for Sunday lunch. Jack liked going to Marco's for Sunday lunch. Marco's mum cooked very good lasagne.

He also liked the way Maria Philpott talked. Although she had lived in England for twenty years, she spoke with an Italian accent. It gave everything an exotic feel. 'Didcot' sounded quite charming. 'Washing up liquid' was better in every way. And she did something delightful with the name 'Jack'.

After lunch, though, Marco started getting one of his moods.

It was raining hard, and Marco said he was fed up with computer games. He was fed up with television. He was fed up with magazines. And all the books and games and DVDs in the house. "I want to go out," he said, gazing at the window.

"It's raining," said Jack.

"So?" said Marco.

"We'd get wet."

"So?"

"All right," said Jack. "Where do you want to go?"

"St Luke's," said Marco.

"Why?" said Jack.

"I've never been to St Luke's."

Marco's dad dropped them off.

"Here we are!" said Jack. "St Luke's College!" He spoke brightly, but he did not feel so bright. He wasn't quite sure why. Somehow he felt Luke's was *his* territory, and he didn't really want Marco there.

But Marco was looking more cheerful already.

Jack led the way in. There was no 'College closed' sign in the entrance.

"We have very good porters here," said Jack, nodding towards the porters' lodge. Marco peered respectfully into the lodge.

They stepped into Front Quad.

"This is Front Quad," said Jack. "It's called Front Quad because it's the quad at the front."

Marco gazed around, impressed. Then he frowned slightly. "Um, Jack?"

"Yes," said Jack.

"Is a quad anything to do with quad bikes?"

"No," said Jack.

Marco nodded. "I thought it wasn't."

Jack laughed.

Suddenly he felt better.

He was *glad* Marco had come to the college. It was *mean* to be mean about Luke's. "There's lots more!" he cried. "Another quad and some cloisters! And an anti-chapel and a chapel. *And* an old library!"

"Cool!" said Marco. They walked through the arch into Ox Quad. The rain had more or less stopped now, and several people were walking through the quad.

Marco looked at them. "Are they Luke's people?"

"Yes, I think so."

"Wow, they look clever!" Marco goggled at them. "He looks clever, and she looks clever and he looks *really* clever!" His eyes fell on Maisie, who was trotting past. "*Look!*" he cried, pointing. "Even the *cat* looks clever!"

Maisie shot him a green-eyed glance, and went on her way.

A plump, friendly-looking woman was making her way through the quad.

"She doesn't look so clever," said Marco.

Jack followed his gaze. "She's professor of astrophysics."

"Oh."

"So this is Ox Quad," Jack explained. "And there's the ox." He pointed up to the stone relief.

Marco followed his gaze. "An ox...?"

"Yes. Nice face, isn't it?"

"Hmm." Marco frowned. "I'm not sure I know what an ox *is*."

Jack repeated what Mum and Aunt Polly had said.

"Oof!" said Marco.

"I know," said Jack.

Marco thought. "Hey!" he said.

"What?"

"I was the ox in our school nativity play!"

"So?"

"I'm not sure I'd have taken the part if I'd known!"

"It's only *acting*, Marco!"

There was silence.

Then Marco said, "Well, what's a wild ox?"

"A *wild* ox?" said Jack.

"Yes," said Marco. "I was watching this nature programme, and there was something called a wild ox."

"Really?"

"Yes. With horns."

"Hmm," said Jack.

They looked at each other.

"But how can it get like that in the wild?" said Marco.

There was silence.

"The horns…?" said Marco.

There was another silence.

"Oh, never mind!" said Jack. "Let's go on! There's lots to see!"

He could not show Marco all he wanted, because barriers had been put up at one or two points in the college. They could get through to the cloisters, though.

"Here they are, the famous cloisters!" said Jack with a sweep of his arm. "You can go all the way round without getting wet."

"Hey!" Marco's eyes lit up. "This is like *Friars of Doom*!"

"What?"

"*Friars of Doom*! You must know *Friars of Doom*!"

"No," said Jack.

Marco pointed to the grass square. "It's quicker to go across the middle, but you're more likely to be spotted. The best place to hide is the well. But you need a rope, so I'll tell you where to find it.

The laundry basket—" Suddenly he broke off.

"Yes?" said Jack. "What *about* the laundry basket?"

Marco gripped his arm, and stared into his eyes. Jack wished he wouldn't get quite so excited about computer games.

Marco spoke, in a low urgent tone. "Don't look behind you!"

26

Kate Again

Jack did not look behind him.

He froze.

"What is it?" he whispered to Marco.

"It's her!" said Marco.

"Who?"

"You know...*her*!" said Marco.

And then Jack spun round.

And it *was* her.

It was Kate.

The bicycle thief herself!

Jack looked at her in shock.

Kate was in St Luke's.

What was more, she was wearing the same yellow
raincoat he had seen her steal the bike in!

"Hi there!" She had seen them, and was walking over!

Aaargh!

Too late to hide!

Though why should *he* hide?

Suddenly a nasty thought struck him. Maybe she had designs on St Luke's bikes!

Kate reached them, smiling. She was holding a camera in her hand.

Before she could say anything, Jack said, "Did you know Luke's has a tracking device for all its bikes?"

"No!" said Kate brightly. "What a fantastic idea!"

"It's high-tech," he said. "Very high-tech! It operates from…up there!" Jack pointed to the top of the Founder's Tower, and instantly wished he'd chosen something more modern. The Founder's Tower looked medieval (mainly because the Founder's Tower *was* medieval).

"Great!" Kate sounded a bit less enthusiastic.

"So it's no good stealing St Luke's bikes!" said Jack.

"No good at all!" Marco echoed beside him.

Kate glanced from one to the other with a frown. "Look, I know you lost a bike and all that, but why are you talking like this?"

Jack looked at the freckles around her nose.

"*You* know…" he said.

"No. What?"

135

"I know about you!" he said.

"What? What do you know about me?"

He looked at her. "Am I going to have to spell it out?"

She met his eye. "I think you are, yes."

"You steal bikes," he said simply.

"*What?*" she screamed. "*What* did you say?"

A woman student walking by looked at them sharply.

If Kate was a bike thief, Jack thought, she was a very good actress. And a doubt began to flicker. "I *saw* you!" he said. "You took a bike from a hedge by the restaurant!"

"*When?*" said Kate.

"Well…it must have been…Thursday evening."

There was a pause.

And suddenly Kate started laughing.

"It's not funny!" said Jack. "I've caught you red-handed, and you start laughing!"

"Oh, Jack!" she said.

"Why…what is it?"

"That wasn't me stealing a bike, you saw! That was me and my friend Clare coming back from town!"

"What?"

"That's what we do when we're in a hurry and we've only got Clare's bike!"

"What do you mean?"

136

"Well, we take it in turns, one person walking and the other riding. You bike each time about three times as far as you walk!" Kate paused. "It's easiest if you have telegraph poles."

"I *sort* of see how it works..." said Jack.

"But is it really faster?" Marco still looked suspicious. "After all, someone is always at walking pace."

Kate thought. "Yes," she said. "But the point is, you don't have to walk so far."

"But..." Marco fell silent.

Jack was thinking about what he had seen. Could Kate's explanation really account for what he'd seen? The more he thought about it, the more Kate's story seemed to check out.

"OK..." he said slowly. "But why were you in such a hurry?"

"We just wanted to see if someone was dead or not."

"*What?*" said Jack.

"TV!" she said.

"Oh." Jack breathed out. "Well...*OK.*"

"Is that it?" said Kate. "Aren't you going to say sorry? It's not nice to be accused of stealing!"

"Well, it did seem..." Jack looked at Kate's face. "All right. I'm sorry!"

But Marco was still not convinced. "So what are

you doing here?" he said. "Why are you in Luke's?" He seemed very possessive of a college he'd only been in for fifteen minutes.

Kate looked at him. "Why am I in St Luke's?"

"Yes!"

"Well," said Kate. "This college is open on Sunday afternoon to members of the public. This is Sunday afternoon, and I am a member of the public."

Marco looked as though he wanted to argue, but couldn't find the weak spot.

"Though in fact, what I'm doing is this." Kate held up the camera. "I'm taking photographs for a school project!"

"Really?" said Jack.

"Yes!" Kate smiled. "I'm calling it 'Views of an Oxford College'!"

There was silence.

Then Marco spoke. "Is your project supposed to be original?"

"Yes. Of course!"

"Well, how shall I put this…?" Marco showed his teeth in a smile. "Did you know Luke's is one of the most photographed colleges in Oxford? And Oxford is one of the most photographed cities in England? And England is one of the most photographed countries on the planet?" Marco was in his stride now. "And Earth, as far as we know, is one of the most photographed planets in the Universe?"

Kate looked at him.

"So there's no way – *no way* – your project's going to be original!"

Kate hesitated, but only for a second. "OK. Maybe photographs of an Oxford college aren't exactly original!"

"No," said Marco.

"But I'm going to do them in an original way."

"Oh, yuh?" said Marco. "How?"

"Well…" Kate looked towards the sky. "It was raining when I arrived. That's different. You don't often get rainy pictures of Oxford colleges. They've all got blue skies. Or snow. And I'm not just taking the famous parts either. I'll do less well-known bits of the college as well. And unusual shots."

"Hmm…" Marco didn't look convinced.

"Smile!" Kate suddenly put her camera to her eye, and clicked. Then she looked at a screen in her camera and laughed. "That," she said, "was definitely an unusual shot!"

27

Written in Red

Andrew Baker smiled round at his tutor group. He liked this lot. They were keen. They were bright. They worked hard.

"Anyone got any ideas about this passage? Michelle?"

Michelle shook back her dark hair. "I think Homer is trying to slow the pace here. After all the excitement of the battle."

"Mmm." Andrew Baker smiled at her. Michelle had come from a tough school, which didn't even do classics, but she was an excellent student. He'd be disappointed if she didn't get a first in her exams. "And what about the language?"

"Well, it's a straightforward account of a doctor treating a wounded soldier."

"That word pharmaka. What does it mean, anyone?"

Charlie flung out an arm. "Here it's a medicine. But in the Odyssey it's the magic drug with which Circe turns the men into pigs."

"Why she bothered, I can't think!" muttered Anne (who had just broken up with her boyfriend).

"I'm sure it's a poison somewhere else," said Michelle. "A serpent's poison."

"I suppose we get pharmacy from pharmaka," said Charlie.

"Of course!" said Anne.

"And in fact the same word is found in the New Testament, meaning sorcery." Andrew Baker picked up his Greek New Testament, and started flicking through it. "Or the black arts."

At that moment a paper fell out.

It fluttered down and landed, face up, in the middle of the floor.

Everyone looked at it. Everyone saw the red letters.

They were bright, that tutor group.

They knew at once what they were seeing.

Chi, xi, sigma.

Six hundred and sixty-six.

The Number of the Beast.

28

Written in Black

"Not again?" said Aunt Polly.

"Afraid so!" Mum brought the last plate over, and sat down.

"But *how*?" said Jack, munching.

"Well, this time they went into some college rooms."

"Oh, dear!" said Aunt Polly.

"So what happened?" said Jack.

Mum told them about the paper falling on the floor in the professor's tutorial.

Jack frowned. "Fell out of a Bible, did you say?"

"Yes." Mum gave Carrie a mug of water.

"Which bit of the Bible?" asked Jack.

Mum shot him a look. "Someone else asked that. It was Revelation."

"Hmm," said Jack. "Professor Baker's written a book about Revelation."

"Strange, that," said Mum. "It's off his subject, really."

"But how did they get in?" asked Jack.

"We're not sure. Perhaps through the window. Or maybe they had a duplicate key. But most likely they slipped in at the weekend. The professor was in college, working on a lecture, and left his room for a minute." Mum sighed. "We keep telling them to lock up every single time…"

Jack started his last fish finger.

Mum glanced at Carrie's plate. "Go on, Carrie, eat that carrot! You like carrot."

"Don't like tarrot!" said Carrie. And she started picking it up, and throwing it on the floor.

"So the red letter writer's struck again!" said Marco.

"Yup!" Jack wobbled the flex of the telephone. "Right in Professor Baker's rooms!"

"Well, you know my theory."

"No."

"My *mad professor* theory."

"It's a rubbish theory."

"OK," said Marco. "But I have a serious question."

"What?" said Jack.

"What was Professor Baker's tutorial *on*?"

"Homer," said Jack.

"Homer *Simpson*?"

"No, not Homer *Simpson*!" said Jack. "Homer the great poet!" (Jack had been talking to Mum.)

"Homer the great poet..."

"He wrote the Iliad," said Jack.

"Ah."

"And the Odyssey."

"Right. Definitely not Homer Simpson then..."

Peter Rabbit went for a ride that evening.

Jack had been meaning to dig out his old train set for ages.

The engine was fine. And there was plenty of rolling stock. But most of the track had gone missing. There was only enough to make one circle.

He set it up by 'Buck House', watched by Carrie.

Then he put the engine on the track, and moved the switch. It started like a dream. *Trundle, trundle, click! Trundle, trundle, click!*

He hitched a wagon to the engine, then turned to Carrie. "Right! Try Peter in the wagon!"

Her eyes lit up.

She grabbed Peter, and stuffed him in the wagon. It was a neat fit.

Jack switched on again, and off went the wagon, complete with passenger. Carrie squealed with delight.

"Bye bye, Petah!" she called, waving. "Bye bye!"
Even before she finished speaking, Peter was on the
way back. "Allo, Petah!"

Then he was away again!

Back again!

Away again!

Back again!

One second you got his ears from the back!

Next second you got his cars from the front!

Ears from the back!

Ears from the front!

Trundle, trundle, click! Trundle, trundle, click!

Carrie was entranced. "Bye bye, Petah!" she kept
calling. "Allo, Petah! Bye bye, Petah!"

Jack watched the rabbit's progress. Or rather, lack
of progress.

Peter was going round and round in circles.

He was not getting anywhere.

A bit like him, thought Jack.

He had not found his bike. Every since it had gone,
he'd searched for it in the streets of Oxford and on
internet auction sites. But he hadn't found it.

And though he had a hunch who was painting the
red letters in Luke's, he couldn't prove it.

Yup, he was getting nowhere…

He leant down on his elbows, and looked at the
rabbit house. It had survived fairly well. The 'satellite

dish' had come off, but could be glued on again. The outside walls were still clean (he'd varnished them). The windows were OK too, not torn or anything. He was glad he'd taken trouble.

He looked at the doorway, and the lettering. 'BUCK HOUSE' was nicely spaced out over the door, and so was the word on the letterbox.

'LETTERS'.

Jack stared at the seven black letters.

And in a flash it came back.

It was the day he and Aunt Polly had stood at the top of St Michael's Tower. The day he'd seen the bike taken away in the van.

He *had* glimpsed the registration number with the binoculars. And the letters had made some sort of sense. And now he knew why.

Just a short time before, he had carefully written something in black ink.

In a box.

A short wide box.

A box on a door of a rabbit house.

'LETTERS'

Jack sat back on his heels, mind whirring. He knew now that the van he had seen was 'L' registration, and the last three letters were 'ERS'. He didn't know what the numbers were, but he was quite quite sure of the letters...

29

Pictures Through Cyberspace

"I would!" said Aunt Polly.

"But I don't know the whole registration number."

"Even so!"

"And it was days ago now."

"Even so!"

"The bike may not even have been stolen."

"Even so!"

There was silence.

"Really?" said Jack. "Should I really ring the police?"

That evening, Jack went on the internet. First of all he checked eBay for his bike. No luck again. There was one similar, but the frame wasn't quite right.

He sighed. That bike really had been one of a kind...

Then he went to work on 'ox'.

He found some pictures of tame oxen. They *were* castrated bulls, he read. They took a long time to train, and went through lots of yokes as they grew. But there were also wild ox, so Marco had been right too. Wild ox were related to tame cattle, and were supposed to roam wild in Asia.

He went to all sorts of sites after that. In one he read that the American President liked eating something called 'calf fries'. It didn't take him long to work out what 'calf fries' were. Hey, he was learning *lots*!

Suddenly he sneezed. Little drops spattered the screen. He admired the rainbow colours for a moment, then tapped in 'ox blood'.

Most of the time 'ox blood' just seemed to be a colour, particularly for leather.

You could buy a 'gentleman's club chair' in ox blood (if you had £800).

Another site showed a blonde girl wearing 'ox blood' thigh boots (and not much else).

There was an item about a celebrity couple whose bedroom was 'made over' in ox blood. They were not pleased.

Jack decided to get more serious after that. *Ox blood...*

The history sites were the most useful. Before the

invention of chemical dyes, all sorts of things were used to colour cloth. Crushed insects. Plants. Wood. Bark. Shellfish. Walnut juice. And…ox blood.

Yes, thought Jack. Blood would make a good dye. He thought of the time he had a nose bleed down a brand new shirt. (Who'd have thought that bridesmaid would have had such a good upper-cut?) Mum had moaned about how difficult the blood was to wash out. So it made sense to use blood as a dye. And oxen were big animals, they would have a lot of blood…

He read that people in medieval Venice were not allowed to dye with ox blood in the summer months, because of the stink.

"Bedtime, Jack!" Mum shouted, banging on the door as she passed.

Jack clicked on his emails.

There were one or two strange ones, which he deleted. Hannah Jones had sent a chain petition against the destruction of the Amazon rainforest, which he signed and sent to just about everyone he knew.

There was also one from someone he didn't recognise, with a paperclip to show it had an attachment. The subject-line said, 'Pix!'

Jack frowned. The sender's email address was not familiar.

kwalker?

Nope. Never heard of someone called K Walker.

He was just about to delete the whole thing (Mum would go mad if he let in another virus), when a thought struck him. Was it *Kate*? He remembered giving her his email address.

He clicked open the email. And read:

Hi!
Hope you like this pic of you and your mate (Mark? Marky?).
My new camera is **fab!** (One look at your faces, and I **knew** all those cheese-hours were worth it!)
I also attach selected pix of St Luke's. I reckon they are different from the ones in the calendars (so, huh, Marky!).
Kate (v. original photographer & not a bike thief) Walker
PS: I think you'll particularly like the one of the bike-tracking operation centre.
PPS: Some useless person, who obviously didn't know his way round college, referred to the bike-tracking operation centre as 'the Founder's Tower'!
PPPS: We've got a new lot of Oxford Blue in. Everyone says it's even Bluer than usual. Or more Oxford-y. Whatever.
PPPS: I'm on the stall Saturday pm.

Jack smiled.

And opened the attachment.

There were about twenty photographs altogether, shown in miniature.

He had to peer to find the one of him and Marco. He clicked on the image to enlarge it.

There they were, side by side in the cloisters. The light was rather grey, but it was a good, sharp picture. Marco was looking cross in a Marco-type way. He himself just looked a bit surprised.

Jack looked at himself for a moment.

He really ought to brush his hair more...

"It's getting late, Jack!" Mum shouted from somewhere.

"Just a minute!" he shouted back.

Jack opened the next photograph, which seemed to be of the Founder's Tower. The medieval tower was at a strange angle to the ground. It was not all in frame either.

No, thought Jack, it wasn't a picture you were likely to find in a calendar...

He enlarged the next picture. It was a backview of one of the porters, walking through Ox Quad. He was shrunk into his jacket as though he was not enjoying the drizzle.

Then there was a series of shots round the college. Almost all were unusual in some way – Kate had obviously taken Marco's words to heart. Some pictures were more successful than others. All had the time and date printed below.

It was a pity, thought Jack, that Kate had not got the whole of the ox relief in her picture of Ox Quad. But there was a sideshot of the cloisters, with the archways overlapping, that he really liked.

"*Jack!*" said Mum, coming in. "Go to bed!"

"Just a minute!"

"You said that last time!"

"Mmm."

"I'll hide the mouse again!" she warned, going out.

Jack enjoyed spotting different parts of Luke's. The funny angles only made it more interesting. There were only a few pictures with people in, perhaps because of the rain.

Kate had spoken about taking the less well-known bits of college, but there were not many of these. This was probably, Jack thought, because of the temporary barriers. There was one photograph Kate must have taken right by a barrier in the cloisters. It showed the view down the passage towards the tree court. On the right side was the New Library. On the left a row of doors. It was not a particularly interesting photograph. Made hardly more interesting by someone going through one of the doors.

Jack clicked onto the next image, which was of the

chapel, but taken right up against it.

And then something flicked in his mind.

That door...

The door in the last picture...

Was it...?

He clicked back. Yes, he had been right. It was the first door on the left from the cloisters. Professor Baker's door.

It was Professor Baker's door to Professor Baker's room, but it was not Professor Baker going in through it.

But Jack knew who it was. It was Alex.

"*Jack!*" cried Mum furiously, standing at the door.

"Mum," said Jack in a low voice. "Come here..."

30

Trapped!

"So it *was* him!" said Jack.

"Yes." Mum put her shopping on the table, and started unpacking. "He admitted it at once."

"But why?"

"Well…" Mum sighed. "Alex had been doing no work. Almost none."

"That wouldn't please the professor."

"It didn't!" Mum threw something into a drawer. "Professor Baker threatened to send Alex down."

"So Alex started writing the red letters to get his own back?"

"Yes." Mum started emptying the last bag. "And what a nasty thing to do."

"But…"

"But what?"

Jack frowned. "Well, it seems out of character. Alex is so…cool. Relaxed."

"I know what you mean," said Mum. "But he's also a bit arrogant. Thinks he can do what he likes." She held up a tube of something. "Shoe polish! I finally remembered!"

"Ox blood?"

"Of course not! Black!" She tossed him the tube, and he caught it. "Go and get your shoes right now! I can hardly bear to look at them!"

"Can't I just have new ones?" asked Jack.

"Not yet. Next month, perhaps."

Jack unscrewed the cap of the shoe polish. "Mum?"

"Yes?"

He squeezed a bit of polish out, and sniffed it. "That six six six – did it worry you?"

"The vandalism, yes. But not the six six six."

"But it upset some people."

"It did." Mum put some sheets of newspaper down on the work surface. "That's the power of words for you."

"The power of words?" said Jack. "That was the power of one number!" And he went to find his shoes.

The next day Jack went into college after school. He rather hoped someone might thank him for finding the red-letter writer.

"*Yes?*" said a voice, as he passed the Porters' Lodge. He turned to see a porter he didn't recognise.

"I'm Mrs Young's son," said Jack.

Not a flicker in the porter's eyes.

"Mrs Young, the secretary."

"OK!" The porter nodded him through, then went into the lodge and picked up a phone.

The bursar was talking to someone in Front Quad, and didn't glance at him. The professor of astrophysics was walking through Ox Quad, but her mind was clearly on other things. There was no sign of Bill or Mr McGuffin. The only comment Jack got was "miaow" and he had to make a fuss of Maisie for that.

Jack was walking through the cloisters, when he saw a couple coming towards him.

The girl was the organist Jack had met when he'd gone into the chapel to look for a Bible. At first he didn't recognise the man. As Jack got closer, however, he saw it was David Bradshaw. But David looked quite different. He did not look pale and miserable any longer. He looked pink-faced and happy. He walked with a spring in his step.

The pair glanced at Jack, and slowed down.

"Er…off to the chapel, are you?" said Jack.

"*I* am!" said the girl. "I'm practising a new hymn with lots of twiddly bits! But not David!" She looked at her companion. "David is off to the library!"

David nodded. "Must get on with my work. I've wasted far too much time already!"

"Great!" Jack looked from one to another. "But...how...?"

The girl understood at once. "It was me, really!"

"Was it?" said Jack.

"Yes!" She smiled. "I hid his key to the chapel!"

"Hey!" said Jack. "Good thinking!"

David nodded. "Which meant I got my books out, and had all these new ideas. Even better than the last ones! I can't wait to write them up!"

The girl smiled again. "David has a brilliant mind."

"Yes," said Jack.

They were just about to move off.

"I heard that someone took your ideas," said Jack.

David shot him a glance.

Jack pressed on. "Did that really happen?"

At first it seemed David was not going to answer. Then he gave a sigh. "Oxford colleges are wonderful places, you know."

"Yes."

"All these experts in different subjects. Talking...arguing...exchanging ideas."

Jack nodded.

"It's one of the reasons I love the place," David went on. "But sometimes you can say too much."

"So this guy *did* pinch your ideas?" asked Jack.

David looked at him thoughtfully. "Perhaps. Or perhaps I just helped him form his own."

"I see."

"Either way I've learnt a lesson," said David. "Sometimes it's best to keep your mouth shut..."

Jack went on to Mum's office. It was unlocked, and there was no one in it. (Hah! After all Mum had said about security!) He went over to her desk, sat on her chair, and started whizzing round.

He had just done about ten circuits and was getting dizzy, when he heard voices. Then the outer door opened.

Some people were coming into the office!

He slowed the chair with his foot, and listened.

Who was it? He didn't really mind as long as it wasn't...

Suddenly he heard the deep gravelly tones of the Master of Luke's.

It was.

Jack panicked.

He dropped off the chair and crouched behind the desk.

The inner door opened, and he heard footsteps. Two – if not three – people were walking into the room.

He was trapped!

31

Bang!

"So what do you think, Eric?" said the Master, as the door closed. "Send the boy down?"

"Well, he's done hardly any work," said a male voice, which Jack guessed was the Dean. "Though that's for his tutor to say."

"Where *is* Andrew Baker?" said the Master irritably.

"Er…just coming, I think." This time it was Mum's voice.

There was silence. Jack crouched behind the desk, hardly breathing. Now he had started hiding, he had to go on. He was stuck.

"There he is!" said the Master suddenly.

Jack froze, but suddenly heard the inner door open.

"Ah, Andrew!" said the Master. "Come in and close

the door! We're just talking about that student of yours. The wretched young man who's been vandalising the place with paint!"

"Yes…" Professor Baker sighed. "What a stupid thing to do."

"Is he stupid?" said the Master.

"No! He's bright. But he won't work. He seems to spend all his time with the prettier girls in college, or playing sport."

"He's a very good rugby player," Eric put in.

There was a roar that made Jack flinch.

"Rugger be ruggered!" bellowed the Master. "I don't want students who are very good rugby players! I want students who are very good students!"

"Yes," said Eric.

"I mean it!" said the Master, as if someone had been arguing. "We give them a world class education in fabulous surroundings! We work our guts out fund raising! And if students aren't going to work, I want 'em out, *out*, OUT! Let 'em go to other universities! Let 'em go to other colleges! Let 'em go to—"

"Quite," said Eric.

There was silence.

Jack's nose began to tickle.

Then Eric spoke again. "OK, we'll send him down. We've got quite enough grounds."

"The work!" said the Master. "The vandalism! And

160

I understand those Greek letters he wrote were highly offensive!"

"Indeed," said Professor Baker.

There was another silence.

And someone – probably the Master – gave a long drawn out sigh.

"One more chance?" said the Master.

And that was when Jack sneezed.

There was a second of silence.

Then the sound of rapid footsteps, and a head appeared over the desk. The head had red hair, and was slightly familiar. Eric Marshall, the Dean, presumably.

There was nothing for it. Jack rose slowly to standing position.

He surveyed the faces in front of him. Mum looked aghast. Professor Baker puzzled. Eric Marshall very puzzled. Jack nerved himself to look at the Master.

The head of St Luke's was staring at him in cold fury. "What the blazes are you doing there?" he demanded.

Jack looked at the Master. What the blazes *was* he doing here? His mind raced with possible excuses.

Mending Mum's chair? (Not very likely, somehow.)

Looking for a Bible? (Unlikely to work twice with Professor Baker.)

He was quite quite mad? (Tempting, but likely to

cause problems in the future.)

Jack decided on the truth. "I came in to see Mum." He waved a hand towards her. "And when I heard people coming, I just got down out of sight."

The Master glanced at Mum, and then turned back, speaking slowly and clearly. "Do you realise you've just heard a highly confidential conversation about a member of college?"

"Yes," said Jack.

"And did you understand what we were saying?"

It would be much easier if he said no.

"Yes," said Jack.

"Hmm," said the Master, and there was silence.

Then Professor Baker spoke. "If I may say something, Master, we do have Jack to thank for identifying the vandal. He produced some photographic evidence which was quite conclusive."

The Master looked at the professor, then at the Dean, and then at Mum.

He looked at Mum for some time.

Suddenly he flapped a hand at Jack. "All right!" he said. "I'll let your mother deal with this!" He rose to his feet. "Just don't fool around in this college again! Not if you know what's good for you!"

And he walked out of the room.

The Dean glanced at both of them, and followed.

They were alone.

Mum turned and looked at Jack.

Jack tried to explain about not coming out from behind the desk.

"Nonsense!" cried Mum. "*Nonsense!* It was never too late to show yourself!"

"Well, it was difficult," said Jack.

"It was difficult for *me* when the Dean dragged you out from behind my desk!"

"He didn't drag me out," said Jack. "I came of my own accord."

"Well, don't ever hide in my office again!"

Jack promised, and left Mum to finish a pile of work. He walked to the bus stop, and spent ages waiting for his bus. He sneezed some more. It looked like he was getting a cold. He felt miserable...

Carrie and Aunt Polly were in the kitchen when he got home. Aunt Polly was talking to someone on the phone. As soon as he walked in, Carrie showed him a bruise on her knee. "I falled over," she said, quite happily.

"Bad luck," said Jack.

"Excellent!" said Aunt Polly, talking on the phone. "He'll be so pleased!"

"I falled over bang!" said Carrie.

"Thank you, officer!" said Aunt Polly. And put the

phone down. Jack looked at her.

Officer? Why was Aunt Polly talking to an officer? Was it a police officer?

Aunt Polly met his gaze, and smiled. "You'll never guess!" she said.

"Bang!" said Carrie.

32

Wheels Again

It was hardly scratched. Jack knew it as soon as he saw it. He took hold of the brakes, and squeezed them gently. Yes, it was so his bike!

The police officer was quite matey. He said the van registration number – even incomplete – that Jack had supplied had been very helpful. It had led them to a lock-up garage on an industrial estate a few miles outside Oxford. When the garage was unlocked it was found to contain more than sixty bicycles. "So now I've got the task of returning all these bikes to their owners!"

Jack looked at him.

The policeman winked. "Not so bad, really!"

Jack signed a form with a flourish. 'Jack E Young'. Then he wheeled his bike out to St Aldgate's.

He tested the brakes. They were fine. Then he put on his helmet, and set off for Carfax. The bike was not damaged at all – he could tell. His spirits soared. It was so good to have wheels again. And such wheels! *Che bella macchina!*

He stopped near to the market, and locked his bike with his new lock. Even so he did not leave it long. Just long enough to buy some Oxford Blue for Aunt Polly, who was going home the next day.

Kate was not on the stall, but they had been emailing about all sorts of stuff. Most of it very random. She had surprising taste in music.

Aunt Polly was delighted with the cheese. "That's very thoughtful of you, Jack!" She reached into her bag. "And I've got something for *you*, super sleuth!"

Jack looked to see her dangling something black on its strap. "Your new binoculars!" he cried.

"They're *your* new binoculars now!" Aunt Polly put the strap over his head. "You might find them useful if you do any more detective work!"

"Thanks, Aunt Polly!" said Jack.

Aunt Polly looked at Mum, who was frowning at a bill she had just opened. "Talking of detective work, what happened about that student?"

"Alex?" Mum looked up. "He's been sent down."

"Oh. Really?"

"Yes, but not for that long. He'll be back – as long

as he does the pile of work he's been set. They're giving him one last chance."

"I'm glad!" said Aunt Polly. "It's very good of them..."

"Well, that's Luke's for you." Mum glanced at Jack. "They can be very generous."

Jack looked at her through his binoculars. "You've got a spot on your chin, Mum," he said.

Mum came and smacked him on the head with the bill.

"Oh, well," said Jack. "It makes a change, I suppose."

The phone rang, and Mum went to answer it.

"It's for you, Jack!" she said, holding it out. "It's Bill. He wants to fix up some fishing!"

Jack scrambled to his feet.

33

Ciao!

"Oh, Jack." Aunt Polly turned round in her seat. "You know that nice friend of yours?"

"No," said Jack.

"The half-Italian one."

"I think I know who you mean," said Jack.

"Could you say *ciao* to him for me?"

"*Chow?*"

"*Ciao*. It's Italian."

"What does it mean?"

"Goodbye."

"Right."

"And also hello."

"Right."

Mum sighed, and put on the handbrake. "This traffic's bad."

Jack got out his phone, and texted '*Ciao!*' to Marco. It took ages (partly because of the spelling, and partly because of a superbly-aimed kick to his phone from Carrie).

As they neared the station, Jack looked towards the business school. The bronze ox stood beside it, solid and unmoving. Jack thought how much had happened since he'd last seen it.

"Aun' Polly goin' in a train!" said Carrie.

"Yes," said Jack.

"In a train like Petah!" said Carrie.

"Yes," said Jack.

"Roun' and roun'!"

"No," said Jack. "She really is going somewhere."

"But we hope she'll come back," said Mum.

"I'd love to come back!" said Aunt Polly.

"You might have to stay on the sofa-bed, though," said Mum. "We're probably getting a graduate student."

"Really?" said Jack

"Yes," said Mum. "I meant to tell you."

"The sofa-bed will be fine for me!" said Aunt Polly.

"Why are we getting a graduate student?" said Jack.

"For the money, mostly," said Mum.

"Will it be a Luke's graduate?"

"Probably," said Mum. "We'll just see."

She drove up the ramp, and round to the top car

park. Everyone but Carrie got out. Mum opened the boot to get out Aunt Polly's case.

"Bye bye, Aun' Polly!" called Carrie from her seat.

"Bye, darling!"

Aunt Polly hugged Mum. "Well, thanks, Annie! Thanks for everything!" She turned to Jack. "And I want to thank you too, Jack."

"Me?" said Jack. "For what?"

"For..." Aunt Polly swept her arm toward the centre of Oxford, and smiled. "For...that."

She turned, and started pulling her case towards the station entrance.

Halfway there, she stopped and looked back. "*Ciao!*" she called.

"*Ciao!*" Jack called back, grinning.

They stood and watched her bright-red head disappear.

Then they got back in the car. Mum started up again, and they slid away down the ramp.

There are some words in *A Stain on the Stone* you may have wondered about. Here are a few explained:

Antechapel *A room through which you enter a chapel. It may have chairs to be used as an overflow for the chapel.*

Bursar *A fellow who runs the college finances.*

Cloisters *A covered walkway round a courtyard, usually in a college or monastery*

Dean *A fellow who deals with the discipline and well-being of students.*

Don *A university teacher.*

Fellows *The fellows of an Oxford college make decisions about how to run it, and most of them teach students and research their subject. They can be men or women.*

Formal hall *A formal dinner in the college hall, at which gowns are worn and grace is said.*

Graduate *A student who has been awarded a first degree (usually Bachelor of Arts). He or she may be studying for a further qualification, such as a "Masters".*

Master *Head of a college (There are many different terms for college heads in Oxford, including Master, President, and Rector).*

Organ scholar *A student who helps run the college chapel, and plays the organ at services.*

Porters *They supervise the main door, sort mail, answer the telephone, ensure security and do much else—an important part of every college.*

Porters' Lodge *A building by a college main entrance, where the porters are based.*

Professor *A senior university teacher*

Quad *(short for quadrangle) An open space between buildings, usually square or rectangular. Many Oxford colleges have them.*

Send down *Expel from the university.*

Thesis *A long work that students must research and write for certain degrees.*

Tutor *Someone (often a college fellow) who teaches and supervises a small group of students.*

Tutorial *A lesson given by a tutor to one or two (occasionally more) students.*

Undergraduate *A student working for their first degree (Bachelor of Arts).*

Also by Emily Smith

What Howls at the Moon in Frilly Knickers?

e. f. smith

1 84121 808 1   £4.99

"Let's write a joke book!"

It was just one of those ideas that took off. Julian and
his friends thought writing a joke book would be easy.
But hundreds of corny **groan-out-loud**
jokes later, they're not so sure...

This hilarious and touching story, full of everyone's
favourite old jokes – and some new ones! – is
guaranteed to have you **howling with laughter**.

£4.99

1 84121 810 3

Jeff really liked television. Cartoons were more
interesting than life. Sit-coms were funnier than life.
And in life you never got to watch someone trying
to ride a bike over an open sewer. Sometimes at night
Jeff even dreamed television. Mum complained, but
it didn't make any difference. Jeff didn't take any
notice of her, which was a mistake.

A very funny and thought-provoking book from
Emily Smith, winner of two Smarties Prizes.

Shortlisted for the Blue Peter Book Award.

Orchard Red Apples

All priced at £4.99 except those marked * which are £5.99

Orchard Red Apples are available from all good bookshops,
or can be ordered direct from the publisher:
Orchard Books, PO BOX 29, Douglas IM99 1BQ
Credit card orders please telephone 01624 836000
or fax 01624 837033
or visit our Internet site: www.wattspub.co.uk
or e-mail: bookshop@enterprise.net for details.

To order please quote title, author and ISBN
and your full name and address.
Cheques and postal orders should be made payable to 'Bookpost plc.'
Postage and packing is FREE within the UK
(overseas customers should add £1.00 per book).

Prices and availability are subject to change.